Benches

by Jan Watts

First Published in 2013 by
Roaring Greasepaint for Jan Watts
roaringgreasepaint@gmail.com
Facebook - Jan Watts

Printed and bound by Lulu.com

ISBN 978-1-291-84556-3

To Jonk

Benches

Chapter One

It's my favourite. There's the first one where the kids go and drink vodka and then there's the second one, my favourite and then the third where the cyclists put their feet up. I like the second bench best, 'cos next to it, there is a sneaky way into the woods. You never know who might emerge from the undergrowth - a dog walker with a dog or two, a runner, a couple adjusting their clothing, a cyclist who's lost their way? Also you have a good view of the canal up and down. You can watch the angler across the other side, if there is one, without seeming to be too nosey. Of course on the other side of the Rambling Bridge, there is another bench a bit further on, but I don't sit there 'cos the dead lilies. Someone must have popped their clogs. Here's a card, but you don't like to pry, do you?

Anyway, half term and I'm walking the dog and I have my insulated mug with a milk and a dash. No bourbons - I've run out. Anyway, some little bastard has written on my bench. It says 'The Fuck Bench'. Blue paint and spelt right. I'm not keen on graffiti, 'cos it always has weird spelling, so the communication isn't clear, but this is freehand, but legible. I look for johnnies or other tell tale signs of sex. I am so cross. It's spoilt my elevenses. I touch it against my better judgement with my pinkie and it's still damp. If I'd sat down I would have got paint on my skirt. So I walk up to bench three and share my day with a man in lycra. I don't tell him about the paint. Keep it to myself. After all, it is my bench and I don't want to be associated with smut.

After telling him that Steven is fifteen and hates cats, but is immune to ducks and geese, I wander back passed my bench. Still tacky. So I think a bucket of hot water, Ajax (yes, you can still get it) and a stiff brush, but when I get to the front door, the phone is doing a samba and it's my cousin Francine.

Francine is one of those women who never rings you, you always have to ring her. Though in fact I never ring her, because I have nothing to say to her. We have never had a real conversation. Anyway, her Bobby (yes, she is a girl) is getting married at last to her boyfriend. He's always referred to as her boyfriend, but he's 47 with a paunch and the father of her four children. Well, I presume he's the father - they all call him Dad. Anyway, Francine tells me to keep the 27th free and that the invite will be in the post. So Steven and I go off to find my diary. No, it's me really. Steven doesn't really track things down. He's not a sniffer dog. He just gets under your feet all the time and it feels as if we do everything together. He has many cushions around the house to park his butt, but unless I am sitting down, he is at my feet.

By the time, I find my diary in the whatnot, I have forgotten about the bucket of hot water and scrubbing, but I do remember the date and pop it in and think about getting a present. I suppose I must get a present. You always get a present for people getting married, even if they don't need anything, because they have acted like a married couple for years and years.

This leads me onto the laptop. Yes, I am in tune with the virtual world. I love it - surfing the net. I find a site that does personalised heart shaped chunks of plastic and I order one with 'Roberta and Fintan forever'. Did I say he's called Fintan? It will be sent straight to their house, so I don't have to do anything else except get myself to the hotel. Hotel, yes. not church or registry office anymore.Everyone gets married in a hotel nowadays. Quite handy really, because a hotel is full of beds, so it's easier to sleep off the alcohol.

By this time, it's time for lunch so Steven and I share a couple of tins of sardines and I toast myself the last crust off the bloomer. After a bit of a doze in front of yet another antiques programme, I remember the bench, My bench.

The hot water gets a bit luke in the afternoon, so I boil the kettle and find the remains of a tub of sugar soap. I put the whole lot in and get an old brush that has seen better days and off we go. Steven can't believe his luck, because afternoons are meant for napping not walking. He likes napping, but he loves walking, even if he is knackered.

So we start to walk up the towpath. Steven free as the wind, well not really with his legs, without his lead on - I can't manage a lead and a bucket and we can see in the distance that there is some sort of fracas going on. I can't hear clearly because I haven't got my aids in. But there is a girl. She looks like one of the bench number one lot. You know the vodka lot. She is screaming at this boy - definitely one of the vodka lot. Actually strong cider with vodka chasers, I think. As I get nearer, she turns and shouts at me.

3

"Look at what this bastard's done to me new jeans - blue stuff all over my arse.'

Well, she's right of course, there is blue paint all over her bum. But I find it hard to have any sympathy. I mean what was she doing on the fuck bench to get paint over her bottom like that. Then I think, well, she didn't take off her jeans, did she?

I'm now aware that I am carrying a bucket of hot water and though I want to clean the paint off my bench, I don't want to get involved in any shenanigans with young people who drink vodka. Out of the corner of my eye, I can see the lone angler on the other side of the canal wetting himself. Oh lord, I don't mean he was peeing - he was laughing a lot. That's what I mean.

' Just emptying my bucket' I explain.

And I do, and I walk back briskly to the house, Steven a little confused by the very short walk.

Steven is my best friend. He might have been a pug once. He has that squashed nose that could make it difficult to breathe. His little legs work, but only just.

Over a cuppa, I wonder if the writing on the bench is still so clear. Can you still read those words? Or has her bum blotted and blurred them? I decide that I will try again to get rid of them first thing the following morning. No kid is up in the morning before eleven over half term, so I decide that Steven and I will take an early walk with the bucket the following morning.

In my letter box amongst the junk is a postcard of the Manhattan skyline, New York to me from Suz Bedgegood.

Hello Nancy Old Girl,

Did the water tour inside and outside the boat- too late to go up Statue of Liberty - it was closed. Too much red meat. Americans over friendly. Love to the dog.

Have a nice day, Suz xx

Suz is my second best friend and she is on a world tour. New York is the first leg of the tour. She wanted me to go with her. Steven is my excuse for not going. Suz says she is looking for adventure, but she spends her life avoiding adventures. I remember when a toy boy asked her to..... It's disloyal to talk about it here and anyway, she said 'no'.

So, it's now the next day. I had a bit of haddock the night before for my supper with a nice poached egg and it's still with me, if you know what I mean. I have decided that I will do this job early and then take my elevenses up to the cyclist third bench and take my chances. I don't want to sit on a hopefully clean, but wet bench. It will take a bit of drying, because it's an old wood full of gnarly bits and moss. Did he push the moss off when he painted those words? Was it a he? I don't think a girl would do that? Would she? Certainly the girl with paint on her bum from the day before, didn't do it. It wasn't her. Was it the pimpled youth who was with her?

I wave to the angler. Has he been there all night? Sometimes they do, you know. He's got his little tent with him. Well, it's like half a tent - the front bit is missing, so you can see right in to all his fisherman's stuff.

'Any luck?' I shout across.

He does a thumbs up. Well, I think it's a thumbs up. It is some sort of gesture.

I get to the bench and yes, it is blurred a bit. The word bench is not easy to read, but unfortunately 'fuck' seems to jump up as clear as anything. So, I start on that. No sugar soap in the water this time and the paint is, of course, completely dry now. I shake the Ajax all over the offending word and use the brush, dipping into the hot water to make a thick paste of cleaner, bits of brush and bits of bench.

Looking up, I can see Mrs Bouncy Labradoodle with her Polly striding towards me, so I whoosh the water over the bench and retreat quickly with Steven at my heels. If his eyesight was better, he would be sad to miss Polly, because he enjoys sniffing her bottom, but I'm afraid, I'm not up to a chat with the Mrs, who is a crashing bore. She always swings Polly's poo around in a little pink plastic bag. Putting dog poo in a bag is something I can't abide. Buy a plastic bag that will end up in landfill, well that's a good idea, not. Having said that, I know I'm very lucky with Steven, because he has trained himself always to poo into the canal. He moves his little bottom to one side and there it goes, plop. Now with his legs, he has been known to over balance and end up plop in the canal too. His dog paddle is not strong, so I have to lie down on the towpath to reach in to drag him out, but so far so good this morning.

There are some dog walkers who put their dog's poo into a little bag and then hang it on a tree. I don't understand this at all. What is that about? Is it to attract birds or insects? Or is it just bloody mindedness.

Anyway, Mrs Bouncy Labradoodle and Polly are heading our way, but Steven and I make it to our front door, before we are snagged in conversation about the church organ fund. No that is a lie - there is no church organ fund. No, it's always some good cause or she's looking for volunteers.

Is a tin of tuna a good idea for a late breakfast? Probably not after the haddock, but I don't want to disappoint Steven, so I give him half a tin and keep the rest for my lunch in the fridge in the hope that the haddock will have moved on by that time.

The postman comes and goes leaving just a catalogue I haven't asked for, a polling card for someone I don't know and a second postcard of Caesar's Palace, Las Vegas to me from Suz Bedgegood.

Hello Nancy Old girl,

Played Blackjack all night and still don't understand it. Lost my pension. Chips are not fries here. Air conditioning so cold need a cardy. Love to the dog. Missing you already, Suz xx

Sorry Suz, I'm not missing you yet. And there is no wedding invitation.

I check my emails. No invite there either. Ones about mesh patches for your lady bits, viagra and bingo and one from Sharon in Botswana that was full of Botswana news, nothing personal, sent to all her English and Irish friends and relations. Her gap year is now running into ten years. Well, good for her, I say. Better weather in Botswana. Who is Sharon? I have no idea, but I get lovely emails from her from time to time.

At eleven, I take my milk and a dash up to the third bench. My efforts on bench two have been a waste of time. Through the residue of the Ajax, you can read 'The Fuck Bench' very clearly. It needs turps or some sort of paint stripper. It must be an oil based paint. It is not emulsion. It is gloss. I don't think it is a spray paint, like the ones that they use on the factory wall beyond the Rambling Bridge. I decide it is a glossy paint that has been put there with a brush. A big wide brush. A decorating paint brush, rather than an artist's brush.

There are no cyclists today on the third bench, just a man with a roll up. I'm tempted to ask if I can have one, but as I can't offer my drink I decide not to. Do I really need nicotine? He is happy in silence and so am I, but he has rotten teeth and I know why.

I walk back towards the house, carrying Steven - his little legs have given up. My bench is still damp and damaged and I resolve to look in the shed for something chemical to clean it.

I see that the little tent is still there on the other side of the canal, but there is no sign of the angler. It's a bit risky leaving all his stuff there surely. I mean, there is no towpath on that side, but people do walk their dogs along there. The canal attracts all sorts of very nice people - dog walkers, cyclists, runners, those who think they are runners, people with young children who feed ducks and people with young children who think it's a good place to learn to ride a bicycle.

But of course, it's not all sunny down here. We are the most direct route for inmates to abscond from the prisons in Redditch. One of the cluster of prisons is an open prison and all you have to do there is walk to the canal and then walk the towpath to freedom and the city. It does attract unsavoury characters from time to time. Months earlier, I found a kid under bench one. Yes, he seemed sort of stuck under it. Perhaps he was trying to hide, but it was too difficult for him to get out again, because his mind couldn't co-ordinate it. His mates had gone off and left him. He was burning hot, out of it with greenish grey skin and snot and his body was in mid convulsion There was a glass pipe with bits and pieces of paraphernalia. I phoned for an ambulance. He'd been smoking crack. Lots of stuff goes on around here that I don't see. It mostly happens after dark, but this was in broad daylight. I miss most of it, because I get up in the morning. Just an observation, but people who are up to no good are not often early risers. Just as well. Just as well for me. Just as well that time that the youth was up with the lark too and that I caught him in time. I do hope he is still alive.

Talking of ducks, which I wasn't, there are a gathering of them close to the house. There' s Michael and Derek, the twins Harry and Barry, Frank and who is that? Ah yes, it's Donald - haven't seen him for a long time. Geraldine is in with the boys too, looking a bit frumpy. Poppy is over the other side, standing on a log and trying to get her beak into some greenery. I decide that they can have the remains of the bloomer. Then I remember I ate it. They like white bread better than the wholemeal stuff. No bread, but I have the stubby remains of a madeira - that will do them. It's lemon madeira. I am sure there must be a joke there about a duck being stuffed with lemon madeira cake, but it's too hard for me to find.

Chapter Two

The geese are back and the ducks have disappeared. I wish the geese would go back to Canada and take their turds with them.

Today is the day I test the turps. I found a half bottle in the back of the shed. I'm also going to take up some nail varnish remover as well. To be fair I have more nail varnish remover than turps, I bought a litre bottle when I still had a card for Costcos, Thinking about it now, it seems a bit of a nonsense buying so much when I only do my toenails. I never take it off either. I just cover one coat with another coat.

Anyway, I am going to take turps, a rag, nail varnish remover and cotton buds. No, don't be silly, I'm not taking cotton buds - that would be daft - too small for the bench. But then I think the bench does have gnarly bits, perhaps buds might get into the crevices. So I put a handful into my pocket, just in case.

It's been a couple of days since I've been up the towpath. It's been a couple of days since Steven has been for a proper walk - I've just chucked him into the garden to do his jobs. I've felt a bit under the weather and it's been very wet. The damp seeps into my joints when we have a spell like this.

There are lots of puddles and mud this morning, but it's early so we should avoid kids and I have my wellies on, so my feet should keep dry.

The problem with wellies is that once you have them on, they are a bugger to get off. I cut the tops off mine, so that I can get them on and off easily. Sadly, I have to remember not to jump in puddles anymore.

So off I go. Steven is very enthusiastic and starts to go the wrong way along the towpath, so I have to head him off, before he gets to the road. I put him on the lead, because it is easier even with carrying the nail varnish remover, the turps and rags. Running after him when he's frisky leaves me quite breathless now.

No one is sitting on the first bench, but there are empty cans and an empty bottle just left there. I walk on up to my bench. The angler is there across the canal. He waves in a friendly way, I think and I wave back. A narrowboat is coming down from under the Rambling Bridge towards me. It is going so fast, you could waterski off the back. It is a hire boat and as it gets nearer, even though it is quite early, the man in a pink bobble hat steering has a can in his hand. I know that he is under pressure of time to get the boat back to the hire company. Half a mile on and he'll be in one of the longest tunnels in the country. He'll be sorry that he's drunk a can of strong cider then. People not used to the tunnel get into it and often loose their nerve. ather than keeping some pace, they go very slowly. There is a kink in the tunnel and when you get into it, you can't see the light at the end of it. It is very scary. I think I was a miner in another life. It gives me the heebie jeebies to go underground. Maybe I was crushed to death in a roof fall or blown to pieces in an explosion. Yeh, I'll go with the explosion, I think. Nice and quick.

So Snow Goose hurtles passed and pink bobble hat waves his can at me and his scotty dog barks at Steven. I nod a greeting back, because I have my hands full. My bench is empty.

And so to work.

No, I don't. I haven't brought my marigolds.

So I sit down on the cleanish and less messy end of the bench. Is it worth going back for my gloves? Is Steven up for a walk back to get them and then back to the bench again and then back again? Am I up for that? I could take Steven home and leave him there, of course, but...

Having caught my breath, I decide to go for it. Rather than going for a systematic approach, I decide to pour all the nail varnish remover and the turps onto the offending words and to just carefully rub the liquid into them using the rags, being careful of my hands. I don't want to get the chemicals on my skin. My hands used to be the tools of my trade, together with a drill.

The wood seems to soak up the stuff and the smell makes my morning sardine rise up in my throat. Rubbing the stuff in doesn't seem to be necessary, but it doesn't seem to be having any real effect on the paint. A scraper would be a good idea. A scraper? When did I last doing any decorating? When did I ever use a scrapper? I have removed wallpaper in my time, but...

There is someone there. I have my hearing aids in, because today I decided to listen to the birdsong. There is someone moving on the path into the wood. I don't want to have any confrontation with the person who painted those nasty words, so I pick up the plastic bottles and walk briskly back towards home. I notice that the empty cans and the vodka bottle at bench one are not there anymore. Someone is tidying, probably Mrs Beagle puppy with the litter picker.

Steven and I put the extra lock on the door when we get inside. I don't know why, but I feel a little unsafe.

Canals are interesting places. They offer a corridor of countryside in urban areas like mine. You could think you were miles from anywhere and not in a city at all. Almost all the people who use the towpath are nice, but you do have a few rum ones who come down. Sometimes, you see couples having tearful heart to hearts on one of the benches. If you are up to no good and you want to shift along quickly then a canal can offer a straight flat route. Sometimes the police helicopter hovers overhead. Sometimes at night, with its light shining down - now that is scary.

Another postcard has come, so I read it with my feet up. Postcard of Grand Canyon, Arizona to me from Suz Bedgegood.

Hello Nancy Old Girl,

Got a bus trip here from Vegas. Very dry, no rain. Don't want another burger. Prefer the Lake District. Derwent Water looks better on a tin of biscuits than the Canyon. Love to your dog.

Really missing you already, Suz xx

It is just the third stop on her epic journey and she is missing us and she prefers the Lakes - silly woman.

I need a friendly voice, so I decide to ring Francine's sister Beryl. I haven't received my wedding invitation yet, so I have an excuse and Beryl is my favourite cousin. She knocks spots off her sister.

'Beryl. It's me?'

"Hello my dear - how's the canal?"

Beryl doesn't approve of me living where I do. She thinks everyone should have road access.

'It's just hunky dorey, Beryl. When did you last see a heron? Anyway, I'm ringing for a purpose. Francine told me to expect an invite in the post for Bobby's nuptials.'

'Nup...what?'

' A wedding arrangement. A nuptials is a wedding event. She told me I'd get a wedding invitation for Bobby and Fintan's wedding in the post and it hasn't arrived yet.'

'I got mine. It arrived at the weekend. It's on 27th at that hotel. The big one by the roundabout by Morrisons.'

'When I can, I get my fish from there. They are very good for fish. They are all trained in fishmongery, you know, at Morrisons. And you know how keen me and Steven are about fish.'

'It's unnatural for a dog to like fish. It's cats who are supposed to like fish.'

'It's a shared passion, Beryl. I could murder a kipper now. I'll keep my voice down, if you don't mind. I don't want

Steven to get excited at the prospect of having a kipper for lunch.'

'Steven must have the constitution of rhinosaurus with all those fishbones..'

'He copes. We cope. So what are you wearing? Anything special? Is it a hat do?'

' The bridesmaids, I understand, are in cerise, so I thought I'd go in a safe taupe.'

'Good decision - a safe taupe. Taupe is always a good idea. Remind me - what is a safe taupe?'

'Beige, dear, beige.'

'Of course it is. A safe beige. And hats?'

'Yes, it is hats, which is odd in its way, because it's all inside one venue and it's not church. No where is church anymore, though it does make the whole thing much quicker. Which is a good thing, I think.'

'Yes, a good thing. I have a safe brown. I think I'll do a safe brown and juzz it up with coral accessories. What do you think?'

'Yes, very nice. So that'll be what you wore to Sam and Coral's big day.'

' Is it a bad idea to wear the same thing to another wedding when the other marriage didn't last long enough for the ink to dry on the certificate?'

'Course not. Give Francine a ring, just to confirm the arrangements for the 27th. You always have problems with the post down the towpath,'

'No, I don't.'

'Yes, you do. You always say you do. Anyway, I'll see you on 27th if not before.'

Taupe, beige, fawn, dark cream, off-off white, ecru, light brown - take your choice. It is all the same.

So I ring Francine and get her machine. I leave a message and I send her an email and almost immediately, I get an email back. She must be in and just not answering the phone to me. This is the reply that I get to my enquiry about not getting my invite yet.

So very sorry, but Bobby and Fintan have been looking at numbers and have had to exclude some people that they would have loved to have had at the wedding. They have excluded those who they only see occasionally, like your good self. They send their regrets, but know you will understand. With much love, Francine.

I am in a rage. How dare she tell me to keep the 27th free and then not invite me. It's true. I don't know Bobby and her lot very well and I have no real desire to go to the bloody wedding of a couple who have been living in sin for very many years. I wouldn't have expected an invite, if I hadn't been asked specifically to put it in my diary.

I press the junk button and send the email to oblivion.

I go upstairs and take out my good brown dress and inspect my pink shoes and bag. With a little neutral polish, they will do. I will go to the wedding, invitation or no invitation. I haven't received the email, have I?

Of course, it is too late to stop the nasty present from getting to them, so I deserve a day out. I've paid for my wedding breakfast with that moronic chunk of plastic. With postage and packing it did cost the best part of 25 quid.

Steven misses me dreadfully when I go off for a day. I have some ribbon somewhere that came on flowers from someone. That would make Steven look the bee's knees. I shall make him my hearing dog for the day. His hearing is actually worse than mine and he doesn't have hearing aids to help, but no one is going to chuck him out of a hotel, if they know that he is my hearing dog.

The post has come and another postcard. This one is of Green Turtle Cay, the Bahamas from Suz Bedgegood.

Hello Nancy Old Girl,

Missed swim with dolphins - dicky tummy, too much rum punch. Weather hot, hot, hot. Very bright colours - have needed my dark glasses. Regards to the dog.

Farewell, Suz xx

Bright colours in this postcard. The Bahamas is certainly not beige. The picture looks inviting and that may be the reason that Bobby and Fintan's wedding is at the Mandalay Bay Hotel - they want colour. Or maybe they got a cheap deal? I think that the Mandalay Hotel would fit better in the Bahamas, than on a roundabout by Morrisons. Anyway, I might not have the opportunity to swim with dolphins, but Steven and I are going to Bobby and Fintan's wedding. Roll on the 27th.

Chapter Three

Fed up with the bench paint problem. I will attack it with my special sharp knife. I cannot find a scraper and I doubt if I ever had one. So I will leave Steven at home and I will put on my marigolds before I leave the house. I will carry my special knife, blade down, to the bench and scrap away as much gunge as I can and put the gunk into the plastic bag that I have in my pocket. I am not wearing my aids so if there are any noises, I won't hear them.

I have resolved to go and do a recce in the woods when the ground is drier. I will wear my hearing aids on that occasion, because I may need to do a runner. I will also take my mobile phone thingy with me, just in case I get in there and fancy doing some online shopping. This is a joke.

I trot up the towpath - no one at bench one. No debris. The angler is there. I think he is mouthing 'nice day' which it isn't, being very dank. Hopefully good for scraping. I send a cheerful wave across the water. Today, the blue paint looks wrinkled. I don't waste a minute and start scraping. It comes off like butter. I've done it. I scamper home. Steven greets me with a tin of mackerel in his mouth. He can't read it is mackerel in tomato sauce. Not his favourite.

The new day that starts with a gorgeous sunrise across the field at the back of the house. The sky is blue. There is a heavy dew, so I wait until later for the walk into the wood.

Am I nervous about walking into the wood? Not usually. Steven and I like the walk and though we don't take that route daily, we certainly do it regularly a couple of times a week when it's dry. We do it more often in spring when the bluebells are out, because it is just lovely. That hint of hyacinth in the air that you get is just so... Well, I like it very much.

The wood is full of earthy smells and then, of course, there is the body. Again, I am joking. In the field from the other side of the wood, there is a stream that goes down to the river. When you pass one of the trees on the further bank, there is a disgusting smell. It is not from the tree, but from somewhere around it. There is always this funny smell. A smell of what? I really don't know, but it attacks my nostrils every time. And then I carry on walking and I forget about it. And it's not just me who smells it. Mr Fat Dalmation With Brown Spots sniffs it too, but he says it's just drains. As Gervais, the dog, smells anyway and Mr Fat Dalmation seems impervious to the dog's pong, I'm not sure I have any faith in his nasal passages.

The walk this morning is an expedition. I have changed my mind, I am going to take Steven with me, because if anyone attacks me, he will suck them to death. Suck, because he has no teeth. He would bark until he was hoarse with laryngitis. I don't know any of this. Steven is a gentle clever old boy (he does pooh in the canal and that's clever) who loves me, but I'm not sure that he has danger instincts. He is no police German Shepherd, though I suspect he would have made an excellent sniffer dog, because sniffing is his preferred activity.

So, I have my mobile at the ready in the top pocket of my kaftan, six tins of tuna in a carrier bag to use as a weapon, if need be, and my hearing aids in with new batteries. I am wearing my red trainers that pinch a bit, but they have good firm soles so I can run for it. When I get to my gate I realise that the kaftan is not such a good choice. It is long and will protect my legs from the stingies, but it might easily get caught on the brambles. I change and put on a black turtleneck and trackie bottoms, like the Black Magic man - remember him? An advert for chocolate? Perhaps he wore tailored trousers not trackie bottoms. I leave my mobile in the pocket of my kaftan.

Steven and I approached the wood from the first entrance, down the slope between the first bench and the field. The stingies grow tall either side of the narrow path, but it's Ok and I follow Steven or as he is known Dr Livingstone, I presume. The path opens up and the low vegetation becomes less and now it is woodland. The light is dappled and I realise I should have bought a bag, there are lots of sticks that would be good to burn on the stove at home. I have to keep focus on the task in hand. Difficult with a noise from a wood pigeon making my head spin.

There is a decorated Christmas tree ahead. Getting closer, I can see it's a tree decorated with dog pooh in black, pink and green bags. Someone very tall must have worked on this piece of nonsense. It was probably a joint effort as you can make out the different sizes of excremant. Different sizes, different dogs. Most people have one dog. Some have two, but very few have more than two dogs. Christmas trees will never be quite the same for me again after this.

There's an engine - boat, tractor mowing the field or helicopter? No, it's a steam engine phut, phut, phutting and that means a boat. And yes, it is. I can see its red, gold and green through the trees to my left, slow and stately.

When I turn my attention back, Steven seems to have disappeared. I can't see or hear him. I can see no movement in the undergrowth. I walk on with purpose following the path. I was going to try and keep this walk silent, but with Steven missing, I have to shout.

'Steven! Doglet, come here! Steven! Good boy!'

If he hears 'good boy', he usually comes staggering, because like all of us, he responds to praise.

I am walking wildly now - doing my equivalent to running. I can't see him. There is no sign of him. Steven has disappeared. Steven never disappears.The path takes a sharp turn to the right through the blackberry brambles up to the towpath and my bench. I don't look at the bench, just under it to see if Steven is having a bit of a doze. He is not there. I run to the angler and shout across the canal.

'Steven is missing. No, he's not a child. My dog Steven is missing. Have you seen him. Has he come this way?'

I then realise that Steven wouldn't have been able to get as far as this. I run back into the wood and retrace my steps, still shouting, but looking carefully. I still keep to the path, because that is what Steven does. He never wanders off the path.There is no sign of him. I feel sick.

Steven has been chipped. The vet insisted. Dogs are stolen. Delightful pretty young dogs are stolen. Pedigrees are stolen. Steven is none of these things. Even in his youth, he was and is no oil painting. He can't see well or hear well. He has no teeth and has bad breath. He has a gamie leg and moves very slowly. He farts badly. He farts badly all the time.

I get back to the towpath by bench one and I decide to go home so I can ring for re-enforcements. Re-enforcements? Suz is in the States.

And there he is. Sitting on the mat. Steven is there. It would have been impossible for him to have got back there using his own power. Steven is there. We hug and I promise some crab pate for lunch. Then, I see he has a note stuck in his collar.

Thank you for the bench.

I open the front door, grab the shopping trolley and stuff Steven into it. I go back to the wood, calling out.

'Hello! Hello, there!'

There's not a sign of anyone along the path.

When I get to the brambly bit again, I decide that I will go behind them. There is a newish pathway, still muddy, but OK. And that's when I see it. It's what we called in the good old day of feminism and Greenham Common, a bender. It's made of sturdy twigs and has some sort of tarpaulin woven into it. It's a very neat job. It's a bit bigger than boyo angler's little tent, but there is no way in. I walk around it and there is no way in. Steven is getting excited in the trolley, but he can't get out and disappear again.

I am getting tired by now and I shout out again.

'Thank you. Thank you for Steven. Steven, my dog. Thank you for my dog. Don't mention the paint.'

It's slow walk back to the house. Well, I'm pushing the trolley and all that fish makes Steven no fly weight. The angler is having a sandwich. Couldn't see what was in it from our side of the canal, but hopefully not fish, because he was breaking off bits of crust and throwing it into the water. They do that, don't they? Fisherman. They throw stuff in to tease them out. Ground bait. Ground bait - how do I know that?

We demolished the crab pate and then a celebratory tin of sardines as an encore. It is a shared passion - fish. We both love fish. We discovered this mania to eat things with fins when Flip, Flop and Flap disappeared from the aquarium. No, it wasn't me - I draw the line at goldfish. But Steven doesn't.

Chapter Four

It's 27th and Bobby and Fintan's wedding day. The day I was asked to put in my diary. The day, it seems, I am not invited to after all. It's the wedding day of the couple who I have sent a tasteless, but impressive and expensive chunk of plastic with their names on.

I am going.

I am going and I am going to take Steven with me as my hearing dog.

We eat three tins of sardines before we leave. If it's a sit down meal rather than a running buffet, we don't know when we will eat again.

The postman is early this morning and again with the pile of junk and there is a postcard from the Grand Canyon, Arizona to me from Suz Bedgegood. this one seems left out in the rain tatty and it has a picture of a very old helicopter. One of those like a big glass bubble with whirly bits hanging off.

Hello Nancy Old Girl,

Haven't been and don't plan to go in the helicopter.

Don't plan to go in a plane or a balloon thing either.

Regards to that dog of yours.

Really missing you already, Suz

The date and the address are smudged. Two postcards from Arizona with the West indies in between? She's been to the Bahamas since Arizona. I think this postcard has gone a pretty route to my letter box. Maybe this one has taken more time on its journey, though Suz is poor at Geography.

It's not far to the wedding venue, the Water's Edge Ballroom at the Mandalay Bay Hotel. The hotel on the far side of the roundabout. We take the number 189 bus up there at 10.30. I can use my bus pass. I gave them a ring early and they confirmed that the ceremony was at 11.10 or as soon as the registrar gets there. She has two weddings before hand in town. So it does depend on traffic.

I'm in my brown and pink. Steven has his matching bow and I've popped him in my shopping trolley. We are both liberally sprayed with Apple Blossom; Steven because of his stink and me because it is my signature smell.They get funny sometimes about dogs on the 189, so it's better to hide him rather than start the day with an argument. He's got some smackos and rubber bacon for snacks and his favourite cushion in the bottom.

I've remembered to charge my mobile, so I can take some photos of the happy couple. Do you remember when you could just make a phone call from a phone? Usually you could get to speak to the person you wanted to then as well.

On the bus, I realise I have forgotten to put my hearing aids in. Does it matter that I will find it difficult to understand people? I don't think so and I decide not to go home for them. After all, I don't want to miss the ceremony, do I?

Thankfully a bus comes quickly and a nice young man helps Steven trolley dog on the bus. There are no pushchairs or wheelchairs, so we can sit together easily.

The bus passes Bobby's house and I can see some orange girls dressed in mauve   smoking in the porch. Spray tans have a lot to answer for. The house is hers, though much of the time she stays at Francine's, because Francine has a hold on her Bobby and Fintan. I don't know any of them really, but Fintan, I think may very well be a nasty piece of work.

We get off at the roundabout and we take our life in our hands to cross the dual carriageway. I sit and catch my breath on a wall under an enormous sign saying Mandalay Bay with an AA five star award. I feed Steven a little rubber bacon.

So this is it. We turn the corner and make our way to an impressive mock Burmese frontage. I can see a door man eyeing the shopping trolley suspiciously. I dive in first.

'Hello there. I'm here for the Flannery wedding. Roberta and Fintan. I'm afraid I'm a little hard of hearing.'

His attitude changes.

'Sorry to hear that.'

'So, I've brought my hearing dog.'

I pick up Steven and show him to the man.

'He is my ears. he tells me what is happening. He's been especially trained by inmates at HMP Bollockston - you know the open prison.'

He knew Bollockston alright. He knew it too well. He was there probably before the Hearing Dogs programme, but news gets around. I pop Steven back into his warm bed.

'Let me help you with his wheels, ma'am. The Flannery wedding are meeting in the Twilight Room - the bar is open. The bride and groom are not here yet. The 12noon Hart-Smythe wedding are out in the Rose Garden gathering and having bucks fizz.'

'I will head for the garden first, so that Steven can have a piddle before the ceremony. Don't worry, anything bigger and I have his plastic bags.'

'Right, ma'am - go through reception keeping to the right and the french doors will take you into Rose Garden. It is very lovely this time of year.'

'Thank you so much young man.' He's forty five if he's a day.'Ah, I can see from your badge, you are a Steven too. All Steven's are gorgeous.'

As I fancy a free bucks fizz on the Hart-Smythes, I park Steven behind a banana tree and head off into the Rose Garden. Luckily, no one is there except a girl in a mini-skirt with her legs covered in rather nice celtic tattoos. I accept a glass serenely and snap off a Scarborough Fair rose bud from a low bush and stick it in the buttonhole of my cardy. It smells divine -ish and probably won't clash with the Apple Blossom. I head back to good old Steven. The trolley is gone.Steven is gone.

After fifteen years together everyday almost, except for my hip op when he went to a very strict Suz, Steven is always there. Now Steven has disappeared twice in one week. I pour the buck's fizz down my neck.

The reception area is filling up with toffs - women in hats and men in suits. The receptionist woman is busy, so I think I'll have a look for Steven without drawing attention to the fact that I am there for a wedding I have not been invited to.

I study the exotic temple water feature to see if Steven is there having a drink, but no, he's not. The space is full of mirrors, so the reception of The Mandalay Bay feels as big as the bus station. There are louvre swing doors like they have in cowboy movies. Steven could easily get underneath them so I follow the smell of chlorine. There is another reception area, smaller with a bank of white towels. A girl in a track suit and a pony tail gives me a towel.

'Hello Mrs Parslow. Perfect timing. Your mud massage is already for you. Your son rang to say to expect you. Help yourself to a cossie. We have a good choice. How about a basic black? Always flattering. This one should fit nicely. Your size. Wide straps, good support. You can't beat a black one piece.'

She gives me a swimming costume.

'Randy said to put it on the room bill, so I will, shall I?'

Randy?

I do my old lady nod and go through a door that says CHANGING with that shape that means women. It's just on large space and I can't see any cubicles. As it's empty, I strip off and as I'm removing my knickers, in walk a rugby team. No, it's Ok, 'cos they all have what I've got, even if mine's a bit slacker. It's a ladies' rugby team. I know that because of the shape of the ball, they have breasts and they are all covered in mud.

'Sorry to catch you nudie darling.' An Australian or, maybe, New Zealand voice.

Laughter and they all take off their kit and drop it in a heap. They are all wearing thongs under their shorts - amazing, but by this time I have squeezed myself into the black jobbie.

'Have you seen a little dog on your travels, girls. He answers to the name Steven.'

'Known lots of Stevens, love and all dogs, every one of them, but we haven't seen one with four legs this morning - have we? Anyone, seen a little dog - anyone?'

They shake their heads as they head off, probably for a shower or maybe one of those communal baths.

I stuff my clothes into a locker and try to remember the number 406. There are two doors one with a sign that says TREATMENTS and one that says POOL. There's a window in the POOL door and I can see the swimming bath. Empty. Lovely blue water with palms and exotic plastic flowers.

And there is Steven - poolside, just about to do his canal trick of turning his bum to the water and doing a poo. I run to him.

'No Steven - STOP!'

It is too late - there is a big jobbie floating. Thankfully, it looks solid. There is a wire basket full of floating aids for children. I take a rubber ring and throw it in, isolating the offending turd. Then, there is nothing for it, but I have to get in. I plop in, taking an orange inflated armband with me. I swim pushing the rubber ring to the shallow end. I remove the turd using the armband like a scoop. Job done. I drop the armband into the paper cup recycling bin and with that Steven jumps in to the pool. I know that Steven cannot dog paddle, because of his gammy leg, so in I go again to fish him out. He struggles, but I manage to tip him onto the pool side. As I get out, a light goes on. On one side of the pool there is a glass wall. The light comes from the room behind that glass wall. Blinds in the room are being lifted so the light is getting brighter and I can see that the room is full of people sitting on seats with mauve bows.

I can see Francine looking like a beige blob from the fuller figure section of a cheap catalogue. There's Fintan standing at the front in a hired suit with his head newly shaved.
He has Bobby tattooed on his neck - why do people do that?

I spot Beryl there in beige as well. Her hat looks like one the late Queen Mother might have worn.

Then everyone stands up and I can hear Percy Sledge singing - 'When a Man Loves a Woman' and Bobby sails in holding onto some man who is standing in for her father. Do I recognise him from B&Q? I don't understand this trend for basques. Bobby's cup runneth over. She has grown six inches and is having problems walking. Afterwards, I realised it is Jimmy Choo and gin. The smokers in mauve follow them.

Beryl said, when she had stopped laughing, that no one actually recognised me. An old wet woman in a saggy swimming costume gawping through the window, was not noticeably me. It was the damp Steven that put a name to the face.

Bobby wasn't pleased. She only heard about my appearance some time after the ceremony when she had sobered up a bit. Francine wasn't pleased. She has taken me off her Christmas card list - actually, was I ever on it?

It seems that Bobby and Fintan chose the Mandalay Bay, because of the pool. They empty it before a wedding, so you can get married at an exotic venue, to get 'the right mind set' for the Florida honeymoon, kids and all.

Anyway, I was there to witness the marriage of Bobby and Fintan. Target achieved. The nice door man ran us home in the Daimler when I was dry and dressed. Steven and I picked up not so much a shed load of smoked salmon from the Hart-Smythe wedding breakfast, rather a shopping trolley full, too.

Chapter Five

After the excitement of the wedding. Steven and I had a quiet couple of days. Just smoked salmon and a tootle up to our bench and back. My work on cleaning it, seems to enhance the lettering. It might be just me, because I knew it was there. I felt a bit coldy after my dip. I used to like swimming, but I'm out of practice. Now I know that the Mandalay Bay has a pool, maybe I'll become a member. The rugby team girls would welcome me back I'm sure.

I have received a postcard from Suz and little parcel in the post. I read a postcard first, I know who it's from.

 Postcard of some greenery somewhere in Venezuela from Suz Bedgegood.

Hello Nancy Old Girl,

Don't know where I am. Have dropped off the map.

Staying in a place just like a Travelodge - very nice.

Do they eat dog here?

Adios haste pronto,, Suz xx

The parcel is from Bobby and Fintan and, come off it, I know it's not. It probably comes from Beryl. Beryl who laughs at me upstaging a bride - I really didn't mean too. Honestly. Beryl likes to help out and I think she probably sent this little package.   Anyway, it's a 'thank you for coming to our nuptial's card', a squiify photo of the bride and groom by an elephant in the hotel grounds, a piece of cake in a box and a chocolate harp (a very small harp) 'as an expression of the couple's Irish roots'. I would have preferred a can of Guinness. Steven and I share the cake and the harp - I know they are not good for him, but at our ages - who cares?

Back to real life canalside. Bugger weddings.

Almost time for elevenses. The kids have been back to school for ages, so the first bench should be free until 3.30pm. It's Friday night, so they'll be bringing down the crates. I make my milk and a dash, pick up Steven's lead and saunter down the towpath.

The angler is there, as always it seems and he seems to have a friend with him. Someone in lots of layers has a frying pan on a primus stove. Steven and I stop and smell the bacon. We like bacon, but Steven prefers the rubber type and we would both prefer a pilchard if we had a choice, but we do like bacon. I think it is the smokeyness.

The bench looks sad. I can still see the words, but I sit down and drink my drink. The ducks come to see me. No geese today. Polly is there, looking more cheerful than she's done recently. No sign of the twins, Barry and Harry, but Geraldine is there, Donald, Micheal and Derek. Deirdre is over on the other bank. I throw in some crumbs. I've been a bit neglectful of my bird feeding recently, but this time of year, it doesn't matter. There's food everywhere and the world and their grandchildren come down especially to fed them. Not so many during the cold weather, when they really need it.

Then I spot it. There's an empty vodka bottle and some curry takeaway packaging. I'll take the paper, foil and card home to recycle. But the vodka bottle, it's one of those half bottles with a red label with Russian writing on it. I decide to put it in the recycling, too. The bin men will be interested to learn that I'm drinking Bloody Marys. There is no top, but a piece of paper sticking out from the neck. I take it out and there is a message.Just two words.

THANK YOU.

I read it to Steven. He is unimpressed.

But I'm impressed though. I have had a message from my favourite bench. It appreciates my cleaning efforts. The bench has written me a message. I have a stub of a pencil in my pocket. To know what to write back is a difficult one. After a bit of thought, I write -

IT'S MY PLEASURE.

It's Ok, I know a bench can't write. I haven't lost my marbles just yet. I know that it is a human hand that has written those words. Is it the person who returned Steven to the front door that day when I lost him the first time. I add-
THANK YOU FOR RETURNING STEVE.

I've run out of space for the 'n' in Steven.

I put the message back in the bottle and return it to place where it was left, on the ground, by the right bench leg.

I wasn't going to go back through the woods, but I decide that I will go back that way to see if the bender without a way in is still there.

We make our way in and it is very well camouflaged. More branches have been added. If I hadn't seen it before, I wouldn't have know it was manmade. There is no sign of life, as I walk around to the other side of it, I can see a fag end. Whoever made this, smokes rollups. Or there has been someone here looking at the bender who smokes roll ups. I pick the fag end up with a leaf and put it in my pocket. I've been reading too many Swedish crime novels. I know that this may be important - DNA and all that. I start to shiver, so I pick up Steven for warmth and a cuddle. He's given up walking, so I carry him home.

Carrying him home is no mean feat. He is small, but very heavy. He's a chunky Steven. He's a heinz variety. Certainly he's not in any kennel club breeders book and this is probably why he has such a strong constitution.

When we get home the light is flashing on the phone. It's a message.

'Hello, it's Beryl here. I'm sorry, but I need to speak to you urgently.'

I ring back.

'Beryl, it's me, Nancy.'

"Thank you for ringing back so promptly. This is rather embarrassing, but they want the thank you package back. It was a mistake. I posted them out for them, but when they heard I'd sent one out to you, they were, well, shall we say - livid.'

'Sorry...what...?

'Bobby wants to renew their vows already, in a Church this time, because they don't have swimming pools....well, I s'pose they have fonts....Baptist Church have big baths sometimes, don't they?'

'Will I be invited next time?'

 'Being Catholic it would be RC - wouldn't it? She, Bobby that is, thinks now that they should have got married at Our Lady of the Wayside in the first place. She thinks it wasn't enough having Father Alberto there in person to bless them. He's been very critical of having children out of wedlock.'

'Would I be invited to the church?'

Silence on the other end and then -

'They decided on the Mandalay Bay, because of the pool - they thought it looked a nice venue and they had assured them that no one would be swimming.'

'I wasn't swimming.'

'No, you were gawping in yer undies.'

'I was rescuing Steven.'

'That bloody dog is all you care about.'

'Yes, you are right.'

'Well, at least you admit it. Anyway, it seems I made a mistake in sending you the package. Can I have it back now? I'll pop over to pick it up.'

'There's no point.'

'Why not?'

'I've shredded the card and the photo and eaten the cake and the harp.'

'Oh I see. It seems they were earmarked for Fintan's cousin Aaron in Brisbane. He was invited, but the journey is too far with his kidneys.'

'So they invited Aaron, in Australia, but not me, even though I was asked by Francine to keep the 27th free?'

I remember Aaron, before he went to Australia. He was in and out of trouble with the Old Bill. I was surprised that they allow him in with his past, but Australia has been the making of him I understand he runs a kayaking business on the river. He learnt about canoes as a youth offender. Oh well, I suppose he fits in well in Australia - all Aussies come from convicts - don't they?

'OK - you haven't got them. I'll say I've got the package off you and that I've sent it to Aaron and then it must have got lost in the post. Some Australian customs person must have fancied the chocolate. It's all very difficult. Aaron sent them a lovely gift of his and her's Aussie rule football shirts. They must of cost an arm and a leg.'

'What about the chunk of glass?'

The line went dead.

Steven and I had kippers for lunch with a slice of thin wholemeal bread covered in thick unsalted butter.

Chapter Six

Is there another message in the vodka bottle? What's with the hidden bender? That sounds so rude. Bender? I suppose it it because the twigs are bent. Yes, that must be it. Who wrote the offending words on the bench and does it mean that people go to that bench and do it? You know - do IT!

Do I want to know about what happens on the bench? On my bench? In many ways I don't, but it is my bench, because I sit on it almost every day and drink my milk and a dash, I did feel a sense of ownership. Well, I wouldn't have tried cleaning it if I hadn't. I hate cleaning and I'm not very good at it.

Has the bender got anything to do with the bench? There is definitely someone lurking around. The sound I heard, the bender and the fag end - it all adds up.

Does the angler know anything? Does he do anything, but angle? I decide that I'll go and have a casual chat with him. It will mean going over the other side of the canal, but I can do that. It would be easier to do it without Steven, but Steven is always my excuse. for not doing things. Taking Steven on a different route for his morning constitutional for a change is good. I probably don't need an excuse, but, for someone like me, having a reason is always important. I have to justify my actions to myself and to everybody.

We leave the house. I have my drink, but also a bowl and a bottle of water for Steven. I also have a new packet of rubber bacon. If we are to do a wide round tour and take in the other side of the canal, then we need sustenance. Ok, I am not going to share the dog snack, I have two oatmeal biscuits lifted from a conference the month before. Of course I've also got the milk and a dash - it seems to be the stuff that keeps me going. I might be old and emertius (actually it should be emerita 'cos I'm a gal, but that sounds like an airline), but I still get invite to some of the dos.

We have a choice. Go along the towpath first and then over the Rambling Bridge to the guillotine lock. Then you have to jump over the narrow bit of the canal and then walk through the greenery to the angler's spot. You can then get up to Bevin Road, turn right into Waterside Road, over the road bridge and then back to the towpath and home. Or we can do it the other way around. Taking the shopping trolley is not an option for Steven, because of crossing the canal.

I can't or shouldn't throw Steven across the canal in a shopping trolley. So it's a decision - bench or angler first?

I decide the angler first and then other side of the canal. Steven and I used to do this walk on a regular basis, when we were both more nimble.

Steven is rather confused at first. We are going right rather than left We do go right occasionally, but it is only to look for someone visiting who doesn't know where to find us. We go up to the road, inspect the damage to the telephone box, round the post box and then down the road and into the greenery. Before we approach the angler, we stop. We have no choice. Steven is panting. Panting and, well, I suppose foaming a bit. I think I am panting too, but hopefully not foaming. I sit on the grass and hope I'll be able to get home. I'm hoping that, in the first instance, I will be able to stand up again. I give Steven a drink of water and then when he's had a good slurp, I open the rubber bacon packet. His little tail wags.

As I begin to drink my elevenses, I realise that I can see some of the towpath across the other side of the canal from where I'm sitting. There's my bench and... someone dashes in front of it, disappearing down the path and into the wood. It is too quick for me to focus - I wasn't expecting it. I am so cross with myself. I should have gone bench first. There is no way I can rush round. I could have done it once, but not now. Neither Steven nor I can move faster than a snail with a leg in plaster.

Maybe the angler saw who was there.

I eat one of the oatmeal biscuits and see from the packaging that the sell by date is six months ago. It's a little dry, but never mind.

I get to my knees and then move one foot to the ground and push up. It's like climbing K2 . Standing from a sitting position on the ground is not easy with my knees. Steven watches, he knows and sympathises, perhaps.

We saunter towards the angler. I've never seen him close to before, though we communicate some how across the canal.

Everything is very neat. His fishing kit is laid out with care. Steven sniffs enthusiastically at the tub of grubs. I put him on his lead and pull him away. Close to the angler's face is familiar, but I can't place him. He's older than I thought, too.

'Hello there, bab.' Very brum.

'Hello there too. We thought we'd take a different route this morning. Any luck?'

'Not yet. I know the canal was built for boats, but when they come through, they stir up the water and I have to re-cast. It makes fishing difficult.'

'Really?'

'Oh yes, and it's better if they go down the middle, but they often go too fast, or along the bank. They think by going close to the bank that they are doing less damage to the fishing, but that's where the little beauties are most of the time.'

'Fascinating.'

'Yer, well it is that.'

'You always seem to be here. If you are not here, your little tent is.'

'Well, it saves my spot. Don't want to loose this spot.'

'Yes, well. Steven and I often see you.'

'Steven?'

'Steven, my dog. This is Steven. Let me introduce you - Steven this is...'

'Geoff - Geoffrey. Please to meet you Steve.'

'No, Steven. He is never Steve.'

He leans down and takes Steven's paw to shake it. I know from this that he is a nice man and before I can say anything, he continues.

'I see you walking down the towpath, but now I've met you sort of face to face, I'm sure I know you from somewhere.'

'I was thinking that too. Can I ask you to just open your mouth wide for a moment?'

'Pardon?'

43

'I think I might remember your mouth.'

'What?'

'From the dental hospital. I never forget a set of teeth. Go on, open up.'

He opens his mouth and goes argh.

'Actually, that's not true. My memory is not big enough and is shrinking rapidly, but I do remember some patients, some teeth. I remember your mouth very well indeed. After root canal work on your mouth, you ran from the chair, screaming and shouting into the waiting room - she's a butcher! It was most helpful. I got home early, because everyone left in a hurry.'

'Oh, it's good to see you, bab. I never said thank you, doctor. I don't know what you did, but after years of gip, I've never had any more trouble with me gnashers since.'

'Yer, I was quite good in my time but it's not doctor. No, it's Professor.'

'Oh my gawd. I had a professor poking around in me gob? Well, thank you, I'm sure. I know someone who could do with some help with their teeth.'

"Retired now. Sorry. Have been for years, but I still go to conferences from time to time. I still get post with professor on the envelope.'

' Anyway, it's good....hang on I got a bite.'

'Yes, I gave you a good bite...'

'No, on the line. I got a bite. Feels like a big one...'

I walk away, shouting good-bye as I go. I realise that I can't ask him about the other side of the canal. He's preoccupied by the fish.

But as I get about 30 feet away from him, he turns and shouts something at me. Did he shout 'Nice swimsuit'? I haven't got my hearing aids in.

Steven and I walk back around to the guillotine lock. This is tricky to cross. I pick up Steven and sort of chuck him over first. He lands fairly safely. I edge across. We are on the other side of the canal. Different canal. This is the start of the Stratford Canal that branches off our canal, the Cesterrow and Hammingbrum.We amble down to the Rambling Bridge. I love this Victorian footbridge, with it's curves. It is steep and often slippery, but with good shoes with thick soles, I can manage. Steven takes it slowly. Sensible dog.

We stop and sit on bench number three, by the toll house for a breather and a narrowboat goes thundering pass us. It doesn't hoot it's horn as it passes under the Rambling Bridge on its way to town. Geoff won't be happy with that speed. Geoff the bastard who turned away some really very desperate patients, fifteen, sixteen years ago. He seemed nice to Steven, but his mouth had been completely numbed that day. At the time, I thought it had been some sort of joke. Did he plan to scare the other patients?

I give Steven another rasher of rubber bacon and eat the last biscuit. A day boat passes from the Stratford Canal, turning under the bridge and towards town. It's covered in bunting and balloons. A banner says *'80 today - happy birthday Granddad'*. It is crowded with jolly drunks.

It is time to go to my bench. Has the paint gone? Can you see the writing?

I pick up the vodka bottle from the ground before Steven can pee on it. There is another note.
Beware of the man fishing.

That must be nasty Geoff the angler. Why would I believe a note in a bottle? This is madness. Someone wrote '*The Fuck Bench*' on my bench out in the open in a public space. This tells me that someone - actually two people have had intercourse on the bench and that one of those people has wanted the world to know this happened here. It is a trophy bench. Someone is pleased that I cleaned or attempted to clean the bench. I know this because I had the note saying thank you. Is the graffiti artist the same person who wrote the note? No they are not. Is the other person in the coupling the person who wrote the note? Could be, because they are pleased that I have cleaned it and that it is no longer a trophy bench. Well, it still is to me. The letters are still there for me and maybe for the *'thank you'* person too. I read the new note again '*Beware of the man fishing.*' It's on a scrap of torn paper, the type you have your fish and chips wrapped up in. It's written in biro and the writing looks neater than before. It's italic or an attempt at italic handwriting. Someone has made an effort.

I write on the back of the note with my stubby pencil

Thank you for the advice. Why?

I put the note back in its bottle and gird up my loins for a foray into the woods. Steven seems nervous about going in. It is quite muddy underfoot, which he usually quite likes. The sun is shining and the light is dappled through the trees. We walk to the little bender. There is only birdsong and the sound of another narrowboat engine in the distance.

The little hut, a mound of twigs and leaves appears to be the same as before. I walk around it. I know in my heart of hearts that this is important. Someone has made this for some reason.

I am studying the bender for an entrance in when there is a sharp crisp sound of movement and heavy breathing. The little hut shudders. It opens up the other side from me. Steven barks so loudly, I can hear him and I freeze. I feel that I have arrived somewhere where I haven't been invited. The wedding flashes in and out of my brain, but no, this time it is not funny. I have walked into someone's personal space. Someone connected to the Fuck Bench, probably. A girl's soft voice says something. Yes, it is a girl's voice. I can't make it out. There's running. Steven has disappeared.

I walk gingerly back to the towpath and the bench. I know that when I get home, Steven will be on the front doorstep again. Beware of Geoff waves as I trot back towards home. I pretend I can't see him. Beware of Geoff? I shall call him that now - Beware of Geoff.

Steven is on the step when I get there as I thought, but he has got a present. A pack of rubber bacon. A new unopened pack of rubber bacon is there with him. He is pawing it, trying to open it. We go in and I make myself a milk and a dash. We sit on the sofa and watch an old Rick Stein fish programme on the box, but my mind is not on his fishing trip on a trawler off the Cornish coast nor his fish recipes, but on the girl who spends time in the bender and who likes dogs.

I decide to write her a letter.

Chapter Seven

Hello Nice Kind Girl,

My name is Steven and I live in the pretty cottage down the towpath, but you know that because you have taken me home twice. Thank you for the rubber bacon. They are my favourite treats. They are delicious. Nancy buys them for me. She looks after me. We are great friends.

Nancy is worried about you. She knows that you know about the rude graffiti that was painted on our bench. She doesn't like those words and she was pleased that you said thank you for cleaning it off. Or trying to clean it off. She tried lots of things, but the nail varnish remover had the best results.

Nancy is now worried about the warning you sent via the bottle and she would like to invite you to tea. We like fish and we think you do too, because you wrote your note on paper from the fish and chip shop. That's what we think. Anyway, will be having afternoon tea on Wednesday at 4pm and hope you can join us.

All the best, Steven

PS My friend and carer, Nancy sends all her best, too.

I can only manage one walk a day, so with this typed up on the computer, we decide to put it in the bottle the following day when we have the energy.

Torrential rain. We have to walk with the letter, but it is raining, excuse me Steven, cats and dogs. We prepare carefully I insist that Steven put on his macintosh. He hates it and tries to turn his head to bite and remove it. I have to give him a serious talking to about damp and age. Because I have been severe with him, I have to put my wellies on. I'm not that keen on wellies. The memory of having to take them off when they came up my calves before i butchered them lingers. But wellies mean dry feet.

When we have put our layers on, we head up towards bench two, our bench.

Someone has smashed the vodka bottle - or maybe the bad weather had knocked the bottle over and it has smashed into five pieces. I pick up the bits and dropped them into the canal. It seems the safest way. We walk further along towards the Toll House and retrieve an empty cider can. We take it back to bench two, stuff the letter in, place it where the bottle had been and walk quickly home.

Wednesday 4pm.

The door bell goes promptly. Steven and I rush to open the door. As we start to open it, a foot jabs in to stop us closing again and this is a good idea, because I would have closed it. It is Francine.

'I'm coming in, Miss high and mighty.'

'Not now, Francine. I'm expecting a visitor.'

'You are ignoring my calls.'

'Yes, I am and I'm surprised you know my number. I surprised you know where I live.'

She flounces in and parks herself on the sofa.

'Of course I know where you live, I've been here before.'

'Yes, in 1976, at the house warming party when I moved in. As you went home, your bra fell out of your bag."

'That's a lie.'

'No, it's not Francine Byrde. Don't deny you were really, really...fresh in your youth.'

'I knew it was a mistake to come.'

'Yes, it's a mistake. One great big mistake. There's the door.'

The bell chimed. The girl from the bender... probably...

'Write me a letter, Francine. You can write I presume. Go home. I have a guest. Go home now. If you have anything to say to me, you can put it in a letter. I will promise to read it.'

'It's tea, milk and no sugar.'

The bell again.

I open the door wide and shout.

'Mrs Byrde is just going.'

And the girl said 'Mrs Byrde... Mrs Byrde? Mrs Byrde!!!'

'Ruby! Where have you been? You wicked girl! Come back here!'

Ruby, her name must be Ruby, jumps over the gate and is off down the towpath. Francine turns to me.

'You have been harbouring Ruby all this time. We thought she was dead. She didn't even turn up to be a bridesmaid at Bobby's wedding. But you know all about spoiling Bobby's wedding, don't you? Get her back here! Get Ruby back here now. I tell you. I am not leaving this spot until you, you bitch. How dare you run off with Ruby. Ruby! And not even tell us that she is safe. We thought she was dead.

Do you hear me? We thought our baby was dead! Not dead, but here with you - the mouth butcher!'

'Now I take exception to that, I was a bloody good dentist, I'll have you know and I have nothing to do with the girl. I presume it's that granddaughter of yours that you sent a photo of some years ago. I don't know anything about her and I left a message for her in a bottle inviting her to tea. It's about the bench that someone has written f....'

I shut up. Telling Francine what is written on the bench is not going to help whatever else is going on.

'You have always been known as a charlatan in the family. What right minded woman would renounce a good kind man to take up teeth - for God sake! Get my granddaughter back here this minute. I bet the dreadlocks were your idea. Get her here now! I am taking her home.'

'I can quite honestly say - hand on heart - that I have never seen her before in my life. That is except in the baby picture you sent when she was born. She has run down the towpath and I don't know where she is going. Honestly.'

Well, I suspect she is living rough in the bender, but I don't know for sure that the girl is living there. I have made an assumption that the person leaving the messages has something to do with the little hut, but I don't know that.

The other question is why does a girl like Ruby leave the comfort of home. I can understand that someone might choose to get away from Francine, but...

'Get her now!'

'Can't do that, I don't know where she is.'

'This is a police matter.'

And off she storms and for once in her life, Francine is probably right. How old is Ruby? It is a police matter.

As I'm at the front door, I look in the letter box. There is a postcard of Machu Picchu, Peru from Suz Bedgegood.

Hello Nancy Old Girl,

Bunions painful after Inca Trail. Said no to river rafting. Food full of roughage. Peruvians wear delightful hats. Dogs have it rough here.

Rikunakusun, Suz xx

Chapter Eight

The police arrived swiftly after Francine's departure. It's a couple of nice young men who have a cup of tea, but refused the tuna sandwich to Steven's relief. I am reticent about telling them about the bender, which might of been naughty of me. Yes, well, it is quite wrong. I just say that I had seen the paint on the bench and had tried to clean it off and a note appeared in a bottle saying thank you. Then Steven had gone missing and then had turned up at home so I said thank you back and asked whoever it was to come to tea.

'And officer - would you like another cup?' I say.

My cousin Francine had turned up unannounced and a girl had turned up on the doorstep at the time I had suggested for tea, but had then run away. I presumed the girl who turned up was Ruby, Francine's granddaughter, because Francine had said so. The girl had run away, because would you want to spend time with Francine Byrde. They obviously knew Francine, because they agreed with me.

The young coppers take me to be a confused old lady, shook my hand and said they probably wouldn't be bothering me again. And then they left.

I think about a walk up the towpath, but I have had lots of excitement and then the phone goes and it's Beryl.

I hesitate. But it is Beryl and I have I aways found her a very reasonable person.

I pick up the phone and I am shouted at. To be fair, it isn't Beryl, but her sister Francine. She's gone over to Beryl just to use her phone. She knows I wont pick it up if I see a call from her.

'So you are still there - they haven't picked you up yet for kidnapping - you evil cow.'

She speaks to someone else in the background, maybe Beryl.

'She's still there. They haven't taken her to a cell. I'm getting in touch with the Chief Constable. I am. Really, I am.'

'Did you heard that?'

"Oh you mean Sir Phillip. Sir Phillip Haynes - we were on the board of the opera together. And I did him a nice bit of bridging work.'

I am lying of course. But Francine doesn't know it. She is a red rag to my bull in a china shop.

" I will come over there with...'

I hang up. You can't engage in any reasonable conversation with Francine. Normally, I might have some sympathy with a grandparent who has lost their granddaughter. Probably.

The next morning it is time to go up the towpath for our walk and elevenses of a milk and a dash. A boat passes. It's a good day and the ducks are happy. Derek and Michael are having a good quack. The twins are missing again and then I spot them on the opposite bank. Geraldine is practicing for the Olympics. She is moving quickly through the wake of a boat that is going too fast. Poppy and Frank are having an argument. Deirdre is sulking under a tree.

Steven and I walk on without much of a plan, except to try and....what's the word therapists use... 'engage' with Ruby.

We get to our second bench and you really can't see the words anymore. I sit down reluctantly - I don't like the idea of sitting on the f.... bench. I drink my milk and a dash. We go to the bender and there is no sign of life. I call out Ruby's name gently. I don't want to be too aggressive or urgent. I don't want to scare her or her to think that I am in league with her gran. Though as I'm thinking this, I realise she probably believes that I am a butty of Francine.

I've always thought that the name Francine sounds remarkably like the word plasticine. This perhaps explains everything about this false woman.

Rather than brooding about this, I decide we will just walk on a bit further and look at the fourth bench. The exercise will do us good.

There are fresh lilies. Hanging from the wire fence, there are fresh lilies. The big ones that stink the house out. The dead flowers are still there, but there are new fresh white lilies on the wire. My dad used to call them funeral lilies, because you always see them in wreaths.
There is a note. There are always notes and I don't know what comes over me, but I look around to see if there is anybody around. No one. I open the little envelope and read the card.

To My Beloved Dai,   I am sorry and I don't blame you. If only we could go back in time, love Mum x

So, can we detect from this note that someone called Dai came from Wales to Hammingbrum and died on the canal side. His mum is upset and she brings flowers to the spot where her Dai died every year. Why did he die? Probably some sort of abuse, I suspect. I put the card back into the envelop that says the flowers came from a shop on the Green and put it back in with the flowers.

So Dai - or probably David or Dave in this neck of the woods.

I start to walk back and just as I get close to the Toll House, I see someone turn down off the footpath to walk away towards the village. Village? Well, they refer to it as an urban village now that it has farmers' market.

I stop and have a good look. She hasn't spotted me. I make a mental note.

She is a tall lanky girl with blond dreadlocks piled up on the top of her head. She's too far away to see if she is pretty or not. She is wearing a thin coat, narrow jeans and heavy boots.

She must have heard me, if she has just come from the bender. She must of heard my plaintive cries of 'Ruby', if she had just come from the bender. It is the most likely scenario. That is such a great word - scenario.

Oh yes and just one more thing about her appearance - I can see that she is pregnant.

Chapter Nine

I decide to follow Ruby. This is not a good idea as we are talking about walking outside my range now. The path goes across the field and this is a bit of a wasteland. No shelter and only one place to seat, a nasty metal bench next to a dog's dropping box that no one uses. Better to hang your little bags on a tree.

Steven and I plod on. I promise him a snack at Molly's cafe, home of the Knortoning doorstep egg and sausage sandwich. It's a great place, but iffy on the fish side.

We just make to the main road and I hold onto the pedestrian traffic light to get breath back. I presume, Ruby has gone left to the Village. I don't know. There is no sign of her right, but even though there is no sign of her left either, I feel it in my water that she would have gone left. So we go left.

The Library is closed. it is always closed, but I have a breather on the steps outside and then walk up past the solicitors, the turf (that is grass) shop and the day care centre. We cross the road outside the school and walk around the corner to the Green. This is K2 for me and Steven. We see the girl outside the florists. She is looking at the flowers with interest and then she continues to walk up the parade of shops. We follow her at a distance, because we can't move any quicker.

Ruby goes into Molly's. We follow her and stand behind her in the queue.

Sue jumps out from behind the counter.

'Steven the love of my life. It's been so long, Steven - there - have a sausage.'

Ruby see us and goes to leave. Her eyes are like a rabbit's in the headlights. I stand in her way in front of the open door.

'He loves a sausage. He prefers fish in any form or rubber bacon, but a hot sausage he loves too.'

' Right.'

" I didn't know that Francine was coming. Your grandmother'.

"Right.'

'Really I didn't.' I adjust Steven's lead and close the door, making escape impossible.

'Right.'

'She's my cousin you know and your Great Aunty Beryl.'

'No.'

'Yes, they are.'

'I love Great Aunty Beryl.'

'Oh yes, so do I. How can two sisters be so different?'

'Yeh.'

'She came to tell me off.'

'Yeh, she does that.'

'About the wedding.'

'You're not the wet one. The one in the swimming costume. Geoff said it was really funny. The only fun at the wedding. They wanting me to wear this thing the colour of a hemorrhage.'

'Good description. They looked awful.'

'Yeh, I've seen the photos.'

'If they don't know where you are - how have you seen the photos?'

'I have my contacts.'

'Right I see. Sorry about afternoon tea. It was all ready, when the door bell rang and I thought it must be you. And it was the Wicked Witch Francine. Oh, I'm sorry you are a direct descendent.'

'Don't apologise. She is horrid. You know - controlling.'

'Yeh, controlling's the word. She's been like it since we were kids...'

Sue tries to get our attention.

'What can I do you for ladies?'

'We are women' I say ' and we would like two full English with all the trimmings and two mugs of builders' tea.'

'I haven't got enough.'

'Put it on my slate, Sue. Have you thought about branching into kippers yet?'

We sit down by the window and wait for the breakfast. I know I won't be able to manage mine, but I'm pretty sure that Ruby and Steven will enjoy it.

There is no point in beating about the bush.

'Are you living in the bender?'

'Yes, it's very comfortable.'

'I'm sure it is for a badger.'

'If you can't say anything nice then...' She stands up.

'I'm just joking... honestly. Just joking.'

I decide not to mention her bump yet.

'So you are living in the bender - it looks very sturdy.'

'Yeh, my Grandmother taught me how to build them. In her garden. She was at this place - years ago, protesting about summat or other. And they all lived in little huts they made themselves.'

'Yes, she did. I remember. It stopped a lot of us going too. No one wanted to share a bender with Francine - God forbid. I question her political commitment too. I think she just went there, because she wanted to talk on the telly. They were always filming there.'

Ruby giggled.

'You're not the mad dentist, she talks about. Tubes of toothpaste for Christmas? Dental disclosing tablets for birthdays?'

'I'm feeling very sorry now. I never sent you even a card. I have never met you Ruby, though your grandmother did send me a lovely photo when you were born. I still have it. You look a jolly baby.'

'That's a nice thing to say. Thank you.' I can't call you mad dentist, do I have to call you Aunty Nancy? It is Nancy isn't it?'

'No, it's just Nancy to you. I'm not your aunt anyway. Call me Nancy and then we can be friends.'

Ruby stands to go.

'I don't need help or looking after. I am fine. I don't need you as a friend or anything.'

'OK you win - we shall be acquaintances. '

'That's silly.'

'Yes, it is. We don't need to be anything except enormously fat. Look at those incredible breakfasts. Thank you Sue.'

I watched Ruby tuck in and she takes a couple of spare sachets of sugar.

Chapter Ten

After Sue's sausage and one of mine, Steven is stuffed. This makes going home very difficult. It is a good thing, because he really does need to walk it off. He staggers down the road, stopping at the pedestrian lights to do a very big poo. I pretend I haven't seen him do it, but Ruby makes a big joke of it.

'All those kids coming out of school getting shit on their shoes! Well done, Stevie.'

'His name is Steven. He does not shorten it. He is Steven with a 'v', not a 'ph'.'

'OK Nance.'

'Careful Rube.'

We talk about nothing. Ruby has names for the ducks like I do, but her names are more modern than mine. It's Rio, Tarquin, Sky. Those names that no one should call their offspring, in my opinion. We don't talk about her grandmother Francine and I am particularly thankful for that.

She left me at our gate and I invite her for lunch the following day for fish pie - I think I'll push the boat out.

'I don't eat fish.'

'You do now. It's very good for you.'

I stop myself before I say 'and very good for the baby.'

Steven and I like her very much. Instinctively, I like her very much, her pixie face and dreadlocks, reminds me of my teenage rebellion that has never gone away. But, I've been around the block a few times and I know that things are never as they seem. And she obviously has challenging problems to face. It might be wrong, but I decide that I will not tell either Francine or even Beryl anything until they can listen and talk to me nicely. Of course, I don't really know anything. Maybe I know more than they do. Maybe.

How old is Ruby?

Steven and I do our sardines on toast to celebrate our first proper conversation with Ruby. Then it's off to Morrison, two buses, for some decent fish for the pie. Steven is happy to stay at home. The morning excitement and walking has knackered him.

The following day she doesn't turn up for the fish pie. Had I said 12 noon? I think I had, but I might have said later.

I have really gone to town with the pie. Prawns, smoked haddock and some white fish that looked good. I wrap it up in lots of tin foil and Steven and I walk up the towpath - sort of meals without wheels. No one around the first bench, too early for anyone who goes there anyway. No sign of the angler, but his little tent is there. No one on our bench, so we go into the wood and to the bender. It all looks good, but there is the sound of muffled crying.

'Ruby, it's Nancy. I've brought the pie.'

Silence.

'It's the best one I've ever made.'

Nothing.

'Well, maybe not.'

Still nothing.

'There are no scallops in it. Couldn't stretch the pension to scallops. But it is a good one.'

Loud sob.

'I've got a couple of forks in my pocket. Thought we could share it here.'

Sound of a little movement, rustle of leaves.

'Thought, we'd share it and then Steven can have the leftovers straight from the bowl. It's a good one and you'll really like ...'

The side of the bender seems to rise up to reveal the inside. I can't believe what I see.

It is Ruby. Ruby sits in a red sleeping bag. Ruby with a red tearful face.

No doubt, Ruby has been living on MacDougal burgers from the takeaway at the top of the hill, because the inner twig shell of the bender has a weave of empty cardboard and paper with the golden arches logo on. It is stunningly clever and beautifully done. It is like an American crazy quilt. The bender is carpetted with something I can't recognise and an odd assortment of boxes tidily taped together make for sturdy storage.

Steven jumps in and on to Ruby's lap. That dog is never wrong about people.

'Fancy sharing?'

Ruby and Steven budge up and I crawl in without any thought about how I will ever get out again.

'It's made with good fish. I hope you haven't got a prawn allergy. There are prawns in it, smoked haddock and white fish on special. The white sauce has a little parsley, fresh parsley of course, in it, but not too much. Chopped it very finely. The topping is not just potatoes, but carrot and parsnips too. I mash my topping for ages so it's good and smooth. This one has loads of butter in it. Butter from Aldi - they sell the best butter. It's probably French. Sadly, it's probably French.'

Ruby smiles weakly and I notice that she has a pillow in a My Little Pony pink pillowcase.

'Oops! I'm sitting on the forks. We can use the tin foil as a little table cloth. Food always tastes better in the open air. It is almost open air here. I love how you done the ceiling. So clever. Ah, there we are - two forks.'

We eat in silence. I know that she likes it. I like it too. There is very little left for Steven, but if the bowl had a pattern, he would have licked it off.

'So, this is where you live?'

'Yes, so what's it to you?'

"Alright, missy, no need for that I have just delivered hot fish pie with prawns in. I'm not criticising. I think it's great.'

'You do?'

'Oh yes, it's really wonderful. How you've done it. I presume you made it all.'

'Yes, just me, It took ages.'

'I wouldn't know where to start with something like this.'

'Granfran...'

'Granfran...oh Grannie Francine?'

'Yeh, Granfran taught me how to make a bender when I was little. She camped somewhere when she was young and lived in one for a bit. We used to make them together when I was little in the garden.'

'Yeh, she was quite....I remember....'

'She was lovely then. When I was small. I don't think she even means well now...'

'Francine has always wanted control. To be frank we don't see eye to eye at all. Never did. She was always the one to be school inspector when we played schools. In the infant's nativity play, she played God.'

'God?'

'That was a joke.Yeh, not an easy person, Francine.'

'I'm not sure I love her anymore.'

'Oh, you mustn't say that. She loves you very much, I'm sure.' But I'm not sure.

'So she loves me and so I have to love her.'

'That doesn't fit too easily, does it?'

'No. It's easy to love people 'cos of their actions. I'm still learning about people I think.'

'Me too."

'So how long have you been here?'

'Not long.'

'It's nice and tidy in here - well organised, but how do you keep clean. Must be difficult.'

'I go for a swim most days. My leisure card is still being paid, so I walk up there.'

"You can have a bath at mine if you like. I always have hot water. Some bloke who put the water heater in, put it on a dial thing and I've not worked out how it works, so I have lots of hot water. Lots of hot water in the morning first thing. Probably too much and as you can smell, Steven is not keen on a bath.'

'He's a bit niffy.'

'I can see that things are probably not good for you at the moment. And I s'pect that family are not helpful And I s'pose I'm family too, in some ways, 'cos I am your Grandmother's cousin, But I'm quite a good listener and I make a good fish pie. '

'What have you told them?'

'Nothing at all. Nor the policemen who came to my door, because to be frank, I don't know much. I could make up a story that they might like, but I don't know anything.'

It took me a little time to stand up and retrieve the bowl and forks.

'You know where we are. I s'ppose we are next door neighbours. Got lots of hot water first thing.'

And Steven and I walk home passing our bench. Someone has carved *'No'* and a little arrow between the *'e'* and the *'f'*. So now it's *the no fuck bench.'*

Chapter Eleven

When I get back, Beryl is on my doorstep.

'So Francine has sent you.'

'Well, sort of...'

'So, Francine has sent you. What does Francine want from me?'

'Well, to be fair, it is me and Francine.'

'What does Francine want from me?'

'She, we, are very worried about Ruby.'

'I understand that.'

'She's at risk...'

'She is and probably has been for a long time.'

'I'm not arguing with you, Nancy.'

'I'm sure you are not, Beryl.'

'We want...'

'Come on Beryl, Francine wants me to dish the dirt on Ruby and take her home. She wants information I don't know and she wants me to join her coven with you and to do her dirty work.'

'I wouldn't put it like that.'

'Well how would you put it?'

'Ok, yes. But a young teenager is missing from home and is at risk, this is wrong. And for a member of our family to withold information, well, it is... obscene.

'Obscene? It is obscene too, for the want of a better word, for a young girl wherever she comes from, to find life challenging for there to be no-one she feels safe to talk to.'

'She has talked to Francine.'

'No, Francine has talked to her and not listened.'

'But..'

'Francine has never listened to you Beryl, nor me. I believe she hasn't got ears.'

'Ok, but...'

'Francine had Bobby's wedding and now that's over, she's looking for excitement with her other daughter Leslie.'

'Yes, Leslie is a nice girl, but she is away with the fairies. Francine has been very good to her and Ruby.'

'So being good to your daughter who became a young single mum at 16 is to demand that she and her little girl Ruby lives with you. Lives with you forever and for her not to decide on anything.'

'It wasn't quite like that..'

'How can you defend her?'

'She's my sister - I always defend her. And what could Leslie do? She had no one to look after her. No one, Nancy. She and little Ruby had no one and no where to go.'

'Tell me, did Francine only notice Ruby was missing when she didn't turn up in the mauve frock at the wedding? Did she get upset when she discovered that the photos would be assymmetrical because they were a bridesmaid down?'

'That really isn't fair, Nancy. Francine means well.'

'Does she? Well, she's not getting any information from me. I haven't got any real information, but I perhaps I will soon and then I might come clean to you, Beryl. I tell you what... give me a couple of days... I'll see what I can do. Give me a couple of days, say 24 hours. And then I'll let you know what I can find out, but just you in the first place.How old is Ruby?'

'Just 16.'

'The same age as Leslie was when she fell for Ruby.'

'That's it. Have the police been?'

'Yes, two young bobbies.'

'What did they say?'

'Nothing very much. I don't think they thought that I was capable of any mischief at all. And of course, I'm not. Look Beryl, the police for some reason don't seem concerned about Ruby . It's the police who are the important element in this. If they are not too interested, then who are we to get our knicker in a twist. If they are not interested then it tells me that they have a reason for that disinterest. Anyway Beryl, this is very rude of me. Come on in and have a cuppa. I'll put the kettle.'

'Ruby's safety matters, Nancy.'

'Of course it does. Of course, how many sugars, Beryl?'

We go and sit down at the table.

'There's a funny smell in here.' Beryl states.

'Fish pie. We love a bit of fish pie.'

'We?'

'Yes, me and Steven. It's our favourite. This one had prawns in - delicious. I'd offer you some, but it's all gone.'

I nonchalantly put the bowl I am carrying and the two forks in my pocket into the sink. I put the kettle on.

Beryl jumps up and comes over to the sink.

'Is that the fish pie dish then? The one you were carrying down the towpath. You eat your lunch on the towpath. You take...yes, there are two....you take two forks down the towpath to eat your fish pie lunch. Don't tell me that Steven uses a fork to eat with.'

'He's a clever boy, but not that clever.'

'Why did you let your pie get cold and go down the towpath to eat your lunch, Nancy?'

'We often do it, Beryl. It's one of the perks of living down here. You can go and watch the boats come down and wave and say how do, you know how you do.'

'Yes, this is very fishy, Nancy."

'Yes, it was Beryl. Plenty of fish - including prawns and a nice bit of yellow haddock.'

'You are up to no good, Nancy. Don't go to the bother of tea. I'm off.'

'No, stay for a cuppa - I'm making one for myself. I'll make a pot...'

'No, I'm going...'

'Other fish to fry, Beryl.'

And she leaves.

There are another two bloody postcards. This one of Pearl Harbour, Hawaii
from Suz Bedgegood,

Hello Nancy Old Girl,

Yet more beaches with white sand. Said no to 'luau' - now living without alcohol. Have done trip to volcanoes and Pearl Harbour - all very, very interesting, probably. Steven is a daft name for a dog. Aloha (it means hello AND goodbye) Suz xx

Postcard number two - man in a grass skirt, Fiji from Suz Bedgegood

Hello Nancy Old Girl,

Men wear grass skirts here. Not all men and not all the time. Food wrapped in leaves, but BEWARE most is shell fish. Have you thought of changing Steven's name?

Moce, Suz xx

Beware of shellfish - she writes that to me? Come on Suz - I'd love the fish in Fiji.

Steven and I sit down and watch that nice Hugh Fearnley-Whitingstall Fish Fight programme. We've watched it lots of times. It's in planner. We love it and just as I'm nodding off there is a knock at the door. Ruby is standing there.

'Come for a bath?'

She pushes her way in.

'What have you said to her?'

'Said to who?'

'Great Aunty Beryl. She's just walked up along the towpath. She's been here, hasn't she? She's been talking to you and you sent her up the towpath to find me. You old cows are all the same.'

'I beg your pardon. Are you talking to me?'

'You told her I was living up there and she was looking for me to take me back to Granfran. I know it!'

'I certainly did not send her up the towpath. After we ate our lunch, I came back and found her on the doorstep. Yes, she questioned me and to be honest, I don't know much about you at all, now do I? She refused a cup of tea and went marching off. I have no notion where she went to from here. OK?'

'Why did she go along the towpath?'

'We don't know why. We do know that she is a very nice person, but is being manipulated by the Fat Controller Francine. You look as though you could do with a wash and a warm - a bath will do both things. The bathrooms upstairs. help yourself to a towel- there are loads in the basket. They are all a bit worn, but they do the job.'

And to my amazement, she goes upstairs and I can hear the water running.

Then the doorbell rings.

'Thought I'd have that cup of tea now.'

'Oh right. Good. Come on in. Go through to the lean to. It's cosy in there.'

'I've had a walk around. Francine saw her coming to your door. We know that you know her and where she is. Stop denying it Nancy.'

'The truth is the day before Francine caught a glimpse of her here, Ruby returned Steven home after I lost him and I asked her to tea as a thank you.'

Beryl fiddles with her mobile phone. This might mean big trouble.

'Is she living around here somewhere?'

Fingers crossed 'maybe.'

'Do you take sugar, Beryl? Or are you sweet enough?'

'None for me, thank you. You need to tell me all you know. This has gone on long enough.'

'I think that goes two ways actually. By the way, Francine may think the police are interested, but actually they are not. They came down here to see me and yes, they did take me for a batty old woman, not a sharp minded master brain, but they were not that interested in finding Ruby. Why is Francine leading this search, not Leslie?'

'Well, you know Leslie.'

'Frankly, I don't.'

'Well, she is a bit slow...'

The door opens.

Ruby is standing there in a towel.

'No, she's not. She's not slow at all. She's just had any fight drained from her by her mother.'

'Ruby - thank God.'

Beryl runs to her and goes to hug Ruby, but Steven is there first and starts to growl at Beryl.

'Get that brute off me, Nancy!'

'Come on Steven. Let's go into the back garden. Sorry, I'm not coming with you now. I'll be a couple of minutes.'

Ruby   obviously doesn't want Beryl's affection. She sits down on the comfy sofa.

Beryl turns to me.

'So you have been harbouring a minor from her family, against her will...'

'Great Aunty Beryl, come on now. None of that is true, is it? I am not living here. In fact this is the first time in this house.'

'That is true.' I pipe in.

' I have had just a couple of conversations with Nancy, mostly about Steven actually who is a sweetie.'

'True again.'

'Also, it seems that Nancy is part of my family, so...'

'Not close family.' Beryl says.

'Not close, thank goodness, because I am fed up with close family. I cannot stay in that house with Granfran anymore. It is stifling and I am not cutting off my dreadlocks for anyone.'

'I think they are wonderful and show an independent spirit.'

'Exactly. Francine's point exactly.' Beryl confirms that she is the agent of Granfran.

'I'm puzzled that they got so long, Ruby without Francine getting cross.' I say.

'Easy, I wore my school beret all the time. I grew them underneath. Granfran just thought I liked school, which I don't very much.' Says Ruby.

'Go and get dressed, Ruby. You are coming home with me now.' Beryl fumes.

'No.'

'What do you mean - no? Get dressed young lady and say thank you to Nancy. I presume because of the towel that you have had a bath here. Say thank you to Nancy and...'

The door bell goes. It is becoming like Paddington Station. That, of course, is not true. It's just that I rarely have uninvited visitors.

Ruby rushes up the stairs and I know who it is.

Francine enters in full sail. She wears a hat that makes her look official. She just needs some scrabble egg on her '80's wide shoulders to look like a Swiss porter (this comment refers to an incident in 1974 - Basle Station and being told that I couldn't sleep in the waiting room by a Swiss porter - happy days).

'Give me my granddaughter back - you traitor! I will see that you are locked up and the key thrown away! Ruby! Child! Ruby! I know you are there! I feel your presence! Ruby! Come to Granfran! Here child!'

'She's upstairs in the bathroom.'

'I can't get up there with my knees. Flush her out, Beryl, flush her out!'

Beryl runs upstairs. I follow, leaving Francine having the vapours on the armchair.

The bathroom door is locked, but I do the clever thing with the locky thing and the door opens. The bath is full of hot water. There's a towel on the floor and the window is open. We catch Ruby sliding down the roof of the lean to. No pregnant woman should be doing that. She jumps down onto the decking and into the back garden. Steven is at her side and takes her to the hole in the hedge. The hole he has been working on. Ruby dives into the hedge with Steven.

Beryl and I rush downstairs. The front door is still open and Francine has gone. We rush to the towpath just in time to see Francine grasping Ruby by the dreadlocks as she comes through the hedge. Steven takes hold of Francine's leg and bites down hard for someone with no teeth. It is more of a power suck. Francine lets go of Ruby's hair and lets out a blood curdling scream. A narrowboat is passing manned by drunken pirates, another stag do. Francine kicks Steven into the canal. The pirates cheer and four jump in to rescue Steven. Beryl is rubbing a hanky on Francine's leg. Steven is thrown by a pair of mighty hands onto the bank and one of the pirates, a damp Captain Pugwash look-alike follows Steven onto the bank.

'Don't yers ever let me sees yer kicking a poor lickle mite likes that agin, yer hag from hell. Ors I will hang ye from the yardarm - understand?'

It is a first for Francine. She cowers and nods that she will never kick a dog again.

As I rush Steven back to the safety of the house, slam the door shut and put the chain across the door so Francine and Beryl cannot follow, I realised that Ruby has escaped.

We go upstairs and peep around the curtain to watch the argument between Pugwash and then the whole crew with Francine. Beryl tries to pull her away. When her hat is thrown into the canal. It seems that it is the final straw. Francine and Beryl hurry away, Beryl cries with stress and Francine cries with humiliation. They don't try to come to mine - thank God.

I study Steven closely to see if he had any signs of damage. I don't fancy a trip to the emergency vet, but I will get a taxi, obviously, if needs be. We go to the bathroom and empty some of Ruby's bathwater out and added a bit of warm. Steven knows what is coming. He cowers under the chair that I sit on to cut my toenails.I sweet talk him out and pounce. He is in the bath. Can a dog cry? Well, Steven can. It is pathetic.

Steven hates baths, but he loves the air dryer. I am wet from his shaking and very tired. The phone has been sambaing throughout Steven's ablutions. I don't answer it, because I know it will be one of my cousins. I go and change. Lay on my bed and have a little nap. Steven does not join me as he usually does, as he is still cross with me for bathing him. He is also a bit too shakey to jump up onto the bed after his flight into the canal. He clearly isn't speaking to me.

'Steven. I am truly sorry that you were kicked into the canal. I was not responsible for that. It was a terrible thing that Francine did. But I had to bath you. You can't be attacked by all those nasty germs. Canal water is filthy. You needed to have a bath and you smell almost sweet now. And you were rescued by that big hulk of a pirate. He was very handsome.'

I have this idea that if Steven was a human being that he would be gay.

I am woken up by knocking on the front door. I am tempted not to look. Francine and / or Beryl would use the doorbell. That's what they used before. They are unlikely to use the door knocker. Ruby used the doorbell too, but she might use the knocker rather than the bell because.... I couldn't think of a reason why she would use the knocker. I couldn't remember what the police had done.

It is no use I have to look out of the window to see.There doesn't seem to be anyone, though the knocking is still continuing. Whoever is knocking, must be very close to the door. I check that I look tidy in the mirror. I feel better than before. The doze has helped my equilibrium. I walk downstairs and Steven joins me at the front door.

I open the front door and there is Leslie, Ruby's mother, crying, almost hiding in the Dublin Bay rose that I've trained to go over the porch. She looked very thin and pretty terrible. She must be in her early thirties, but looks as old as me. Leslie is wearing a pale pink twinset, pearls and a grey pleated skirt. Her mother, Francine dresses her as a clone of herself. I notice that she has on her feet those shoes that are a rubberised plastic that snap back into a curl when you take them off. Very, very old people might choose to wear them, but not someone in their thirties. I didn't know that you could still buy them. In my book, they are an accessory to go with trews.

I pull Leslie into the house.

The letter box is open and there is a postcard, a bit chewed of an Australian Train, from Suz Bedgegood.

Hello Nancy Old Girl,

Doing the Indian Pacific train journey from the Pacific Ocean to the Indian Ocean. Posting this in Kalgoolie in the Outback. Gone Platinium - big double bed. Perth the next stop. Very boring just looking out of the window - it all looks the same to me. I'm not keen on dogs.

Fair dikum, Suz xx

Well, Suz, it's not boring looking out of the window here.

Chapter Twelve

Leslie is cold. She is thin. She is gulping air between sobs. I must have met her before. I know who it is. After she got pregnant, I suppose at sixteen, Francine kept her bottled up. As I avoid Francine anyway, I have no real recollection of seeing Leslie at all. This is a harsh thing to say, but I think that even if I had been in the same space as Leslie, I might not of noticed her. It is difficult to believe that she is the daughter of Francine and the sister of the busty and bossy new bride Bobby. Leslie, unlike her mother and sister, is the sort of person that is easy to ignore. But not now. She is a sad sight for sore eyes. I put her by the fire and put the kettle on.

'Thank you, yes, thank you, thank you very much. Ruby says that you, you, Nancy, have been very kind. You have been very kind to my Ruby. She said that you have taken her for two breakfasts, yes, two breakfasts at that Molly place, up in the village, at the Green. You bought her a breakfast and then she ate yours as well. And fish pie. She's always refuse my mother's fish. It's grey, mother's fish pie. It's grey like...like...horrid. Thank you for being kind to Ruby. She is a lovely girl. She is a sweet girl. I love her. Thank you and please don't tell them. Don't tell them. Please don't tell them. They mustn't know.'

'Here's a tea - I've put sugar in it. Bad for the teeth of course, but who cares. Bad teeth are good for dentists.'

'What? Don't say what Leslie - it's not polite, Leslie. You have to mind your Ps and Q's Leslie. Be a nice girl, Leslie.

Shut up Mother! Shut up, I'm telling you now, Mother!'
Leslie talks to herself.

Poor Leslie is in a difficult place. No fresh fish, so I give her
a cuppa soup. Shropshire Pea.
She drinks half slowly in silence. She sleeps. I bring a
duvet down and put it over her.

Leslie has an old lady's good quality handbag with her.
She clasped it to her chest when she was at the door.
Now it's at her feet.

Leslie and Ruby communicate. Leslie probably knows
where Ruby is living. How do they communicate? Mobile
phone? Leslie is snoring softly. I cross my fingers and open
the bag and remove Leslie's mobile. Password? Try Ruby -
it opens. And there is a call noted from Ruby. I go to the
bathroom and ring it.

'Hello Mum, it's been such a day. Granfran and Great
Aunty Beryl turned up when I was having a b....'

'Ruby, it's me. Your mum is here at the cottage. She's
looking awful - well, she was upset, but she's fast asleep.
Can you come on down here safely? The two witches
might be about...'

'Go away! Bugger off you bastard! I'm not coming with
you.I am fed up with you - go away! Put me down.'

The noise of the scuffle makes my blood grow cold.

'Get help Nancy! Help please!'

'Is it Francine?'

'No, it's...'

The mobile goes dead.

It's difficult for me and Steven to move fast, but we do our best. A narrowboat is up ahead and moving off. We get to the bender in about 7 minutes and 49 seconds - thank you mobile phone.

We dive into the wood. Daylight is going, but it is light enough to see that the bender is open. There has been a struggle you can see and there is Ruby's mobile phone.

I think Ruby is on that boat. I think Ruby has been taken from the bender and put on the boat. The boat is heading towards town. That is the thing about the canals, routes are limited. That boat has gone under the bridge heading for town. I need to head it off. Using Ruby's mobile phone, I ring for a taxi. One can be with me in five minutes. Steven and I go to the road by the guillotine lock and almost immediately there is a taxi.

The taxi driver is not our usual Khaver Khan. He is reluctant to let Steven in, but I assure him that Steven has had a bath this very day. I ask him to drop us off in Selly Oak. Steven and I gird up our loins to walk to the narrow bit under the railway bridge. My idea is to wait in the shadows and jump onto the boat and slay the dragon. Well... I have no idea what then, to be honest.

I ask the taxi driver to put the bill on the slate and that's Ok with him. He just wants Steven out of his cab.

We walk back towards the bridge. It's not a long walk, but I'm whacked when we get there. Steven lays on his back, little legs in the air. He is knackered too. Narrowboats can't go faster than 5 miles an hour in theory, some with powerful engines can go faster, but you are not allowed to because it erodes the banks of the canal. I know that by taking the taxi, I must be ahead of the narrowboat that Ruby is on. No boat can be quicker than a taxi driver in an elderly Mercedes.

It is now dark. In the gloom, I can see a boat approach. It must have been going very fast to get to the railway bridge so quickly. It has a strong navigation light. The person steering will probably see me, but I will have to take my chance. The boat slows as it approaches the narrow channel. It's tricky, because it is just the width of the boat. It is a long boat, probably 71 foot. This boat is being steered by someone who can cut the mustard. It slips into the channel perfectly, difficult with such a long boat and in the dark. As the light moves past me, I see that it has a side door and that it is open. I put Steven under my arm.

Then there is a rasping sound. The engine just ticks over.

'Blasted litterbug. Throwing their crap into the drink. Bastard!'

Father Christmas, red sweater, white beard that looked real, black wellies and a bobble hat, leans over the far side of the boat and removes some bits of rubbish from the water. I jump onto the top step that leads into the boat and then down the three step ladder. I am on board. The boatman should have seen me, but... the boat moves serenely on.

The boat rocks a little. Inside the boat is heavenly. A traditional craft, but this is not the point - Ruby? And there might be lot of wicked people on board with guns and knives and... The boat appears to be empty at first glance.

I whisper in Steven's ear.

'Find Ruby.'

I put him down on the floor. He sits and then rolls onto his back again. No help.

I walk through what is obviously someone's home. I walk away from the business end and the person steering. The bow has a comfy double bed with cute curtains and storage it seems. Then there's a little toilet with a tiny shower room off to one side and is that a washing machine? Yes, how civilised? Then back where I've come on board, a kitchen with all the gubbins and plates in the sink for washing up and then a sitting area with one of those little stoves that burn everything.

No sign of Ruby. No sign of anyone. It is either the wrong boat or Ruby has got off. The boat is moving steadily towards town.

Dilemma - do I jump off the boat at the next narrow channel, under the next railway bridge, just before the aqueduct or do I just stay on until the boat stops? Do I confront the person, I think it is a man, who is steering?

I close the side door to keep the wind out and look at the little stove. It is burning slowly. I put in a log and open the draft to make it burn up a bit. Steven and I sit cuddled up on a very comfy seat. And I'm afraid that we just nod off.

I wake up to a repetitive chirping. It's a mobile phone. It must be Ruby's. I have it in my pocket.

'It's Mum here, Ruby. OK? How's the bender? I'll bring some supplies tomorrow morning.'

'It's me Leslie. It's me, Nancy. Ruby has done what you've done. Gone to sleep I was just bringing her some hot Ovaltine.' I lie.

'I didn't know you could still get that.' Says Leslie, believing me.

'Oh yes, in handy sachets.'

'If I were you, I'd get home. Just shut the door of the cottage. perhaps we could all meet at mine tomorrow morning for breakfast and have a catch up. I think we should. Yes?'

'Ok as long as Ruby is comfortable tonight. Mother will be wondering where I am now. i said that I was popping to the late opening of the library. She hates books, so she never argues and checks if I'm there.'

'Really. Come over when you can. If there's no answer then there's a key under stone on the step.'

'Ok. Give Ruby a kiss from me.'

Chance would be a fine thing. I have until morning to find Ruby and get the two of us back home. Three of us, mustn't forget the gorgeous Steven, who at that moment is licking his bits.

I wash and dry up. The boat has to stop soon. Traveling at night in the dark on a narrowboat is not easy, even on a length of canal you know well. I'm hoping that it will go as far as town, because there will be lots of people about and killing me may be more difficult. Though I have my secret weapon for protection Super Steven Wonder Dog. I'm making up all this rubbish in my head, because I am enjoying the excitement in many ways, but it is all rather scary if I think about it too much in a negative way. I have to be upbeat. The most exciting thing canalside usually is...is... I can't think of anything, except when the nice man comes to read the meter and the coal is delivered by the coal boat.

So I've done the washing and drying up, but I haven't put away, because there is nothing worst than someone else putting things away and then you can't find anything. So I think that Father Crimbo might like a cuppa and might be happy if I make him one. I don't think that Ruby has been on this boat. I think I have missed the boat, in fact.

I look to see what beverages he has on his shelves and I can see that he must be partial to tea in those bags invented by the ancient Egyptians - tea in pyramids. The kettle has some water in, so I put it on the little stove. The space is getting really toasty now. I look for milk and find full fat in the little fridge that doesn't seem to be working. Does he take sugar? Yes, he does, because there is a bowl of it with cruddy bits - well used. I find a tray, put on a couple of tin mugs, the little plastic thing of milk and the sugar bowl. I have just washed up a teaspoon, so I add that to the tray. I am just looking for biscuits, when I can feel the engine noise changing and the boat slowing and moving to the left. He's mooring up. I hear someone jump off the boat. The boat moves sideways. I know that it is being pulled by rope. I can hear the clank of the mooring ring. Any minute now, Santa is going to come inside his boat and find two stowaways. I need to make this a good bit of talking. I put the tray on the table and then I get cold feet. I pick up Steven and we hide in the tiny shower room.

Chapter Thirteen

A prolonged guffaw of laughter and then running up and off the boat.

'Charlie! Charlie! Come and see this - quick - I don't believe it! You won't believe this! Charlie! Come here! It's hot! Come here quick! Charlie!'

There is some movement. I think it's from another boat. I am pleased I'm wearing my hearing aids or I would be buggered. I put the volume on to TV. It's the loudest.

I think that we are moored up at the the Vale, past the Uni and by the big halls of residence. Boats often gather there by a bit of wooded grass. People make open fires and drink rough cider. It has a remoteness, which is silly really because there are houses close by, the railway one side and the canal the other.

Charlie must be another boatman and he and Christmas are meeting to sit by an open fire and compare Christmas lists - no, no, no.

The boat judders and two people get on.

'Look Charlie - see - it's like elves.'

'Elves?'

'There's tea in the pot. Hot tea and it's all on a tray and someone has done the washing up. Look, Charlie, it's a miracle.'

'OK Chris...'

I wasn't far off with Christmas.

'I haven't made the tea. I haven't washed up. Someone must have done it, but there is only me.'

With that my mobile starts to ring. Footsteps. The shower curtain is drawn. Steven starts to bark.

'I can explain everything.'

'Out young lady.'

Young lady? The light is poor, but...how wonderful to be called young lady? What a charmer? I really hoped that Chris has had nothing to do with Ruby's abduction.

'I can explain everything. Stop barking Steven.'

Steven is a very obedient dog and Chris and Charlie are very impressed that I have that sort of control, I think. I hope.

'The water is a bit cold for a shower this time of night. Maybe we should drink that tea, while it's still hot.'

Charlie said 'well, Chris, I thought you were a bit long in the tooth to be stashing birds away on your boat. But good on yer.'

'I am not a bird, duck or swan, thank you very much.' I get out of the shower, past the men and walk to the living area.

'I wanted to be helpful, so I washed up and made tea, because ... I thought that might be useful. Thank you for the lift. I have a question for you before I go. Do you know the whereabouts of a young caucasian girl about so tall, with fair dreadlocks who wears narrow jeans, even though she is obviously pregnant?'

'Pregnant?' says Charlie.

'She is, in fact, 16. She is living rough and is being hounded by her grandmother. There are lots of other bits to this story too, but...I need to sit down. '

I feel completely pooped. Charlie passes me a cup of tea. Most welcome.

'This is my boat. I have no idea how you come to be on it. You have not been invited and people only come on my boat by invitation.' Chris says.

'Quite right too. I don't have a problem with that.'

Charlie asks for biscuits.

'In the left hand cupboard.'

I think you can always tell a man by his biscuits. Rich Tea and they are villains. Chocolate Hobnobs and they are generous and fun.Charlie comes back with fly biscuits, Garibaldis.
What does that say about a man?

'Fly biscuits?'

'Yes, a present from a friend.'

'Not much of a friend,' says Charlie.

'No, not much,' I agree, though we both take one.

'Dried fruit can be quite nice, but it has to be moist.'

'One of life's ironies that, I think.'

We all think about a biscuit for a moment, while Steven pinches one off the plate.

'Naughty boy Steven!' I say and anybody would think I had said something funny.

'How did you get on my boat?' Chris is serious.

'I popped on at the narrow bit by the railway bridge. You were rooting out a bit of plastic and Steven and I got on.'

There is more laughter when I mention Steven's name.

'So why did you get on my boat? I don't think an explanation is unreasonable. Who is the girl?'

I go around the houses a bit, but to be fair both of the boys (well if I am a young lady, then they are certainly the boys) seem to be quite fascinated by the whole thing. They both seemed surprised that I am happy to use the word 'fuck', but it is difficult not too, if some bastard has written it in blue paint on my favourite bench.

'The only intruder on my boat this evening is you, young lady and erm Steven. I've come down the Stratford Canal. I take my time - that's what narrowboats are about - not rushing and going slowly. As I was passing through Bourneville a boat came up my arse and over took me.'

Right, he's come from the Stratford Canal, so he didn't pass my bench.

'That would have been Buzzard. It came through here like a dose of salts. My boat rocked like buggery when it past. Its a hire boat from the Saxon Boatyard. They were taking so little care, I was tempted to ring the company so they would loose their deposit, but the signal here is....' Charlie said.

'That must have been the boat with Ruby on. Oh dear, I'm so worried and Leslie, that's her mum, thinks that she is asleep.'

'Police, it is.'

Chris is serious and maybe he is right, but...I don't know , but I think by the time we explain everything it will be too late to act. They know that Francine is saying that Ruby is missing, but I think that the reason they are so laid back about it is that her mum, Leslie, has told them that she isn't missing. Yes, that makes some sense.

'If you are willing to help me, we could resolve this now. We can rescue Ruby and return her to her Mum. That boat must be going to town.'

'Yes, don't bring in the police. There are no boats with blue flashing lights on top. It will be difficult to get any activity quickly down here. '

'So let's go to town then.'

'Good luck then. I'll untie you.'

'Thank you so much, Chris - I can call you Chris?' I simper. I didn't know I could simper.

We thunder down the canal towards town, lights blazing. Steven hides down below. It is exhilarating standing next the skilled Chris. I'm anxious because of Ruby. Where is Ruby? And I'm exhilarated because I am standing next to an old, but very handsome and kind man - it's been a few years since that has happened.

The entry into town by boat is fantastic. The Cube rises to the right with the Mailbox behind and you have to dive left under the footbbridge to the Cesterrow Bar. This is not a drinky - poos bar, but the narrow channel between the

Hammingbrum and Cesterrow Canal and the Hammingbrum Mainline Navigation.

But we don't get as far as the Bar, because there on the left, moored up, is the Saxon boat Buzzard. The curtains are drawn, but there is light coming from inside. We cannot see into the Buzzard and there is no one hanging about the boat at all, except for a group of pink fluffy women walking along the towpath on a hen do. Chris passes the boat and so that we can make a quick get away he turns his boat at the Gas Street Basin. The idea is to come along side the Buzzard. Tie up the All Day Breakfast - yes, Chris's narrowboat is called the All Day Breakfast - to the Buzzard and we send in Steven barking. Then he and I will push our way in and retrieve Ruby and take her back to mine. Then I will get out the single malt.

It is all planned.

So Chris cuts the engine and we cruise alongside the Buzzard. He slips the middle rope across to the rail of the Buzzard. I retrieve Steven and we board the Buzzard. Chris following. Those inside have obviously felt the judders as we land and the door opens.

'Hi y'all - can I help you?'

The door opens to a large family in mid-meal. Burgers from the gourmet burger place along the towpath, I think.

'Ah, Americans?' I say.

'Sorry ma'am, we are from Canada, not the US.' Says Pa.

The little children, and there seem to be lots of them, looked eagerly at Steven and make ah sounds.

'Ruby? Is Ruby here?, please.'

'Ruby, no, we have a Tammy, a Joy, a Betty, a Dorothy and a Merrilyn, but no Ruby. '

'I am from the Saxon Boat Hire people, sorry to disturb you all on your holiday, but I have been sent out to check up on the Muzzle Gurgle System. There are concerns. I'll just go for'ard to check.' Chris looks so important that no one asks for his credentials.

'What wonderful teeth you Canadians have, before I became a inspector for Saxon, I was a dentist.' I jabber.

Chris comes back from the inner reaches of the boat shaking his head. No Ruby then.

'The Muzzle Gurgler seems fine on this boat, but be careful to top up the system at regular intervals with elbow grease.'

We leave sharpish and untie the All Day Breakfast and head off out of town. We manage to avoid the boy being sick over the side of the footbridge and we head back towards the Vale, back where we came from.

'How well do you know, Charlie?' I ask.

'Not very well. There are a group of boaters who get together at the Vale once a month if they are in the area. We light a fire and tell stories, someone usually has a guitar and maybe we have a bit too much cider. He's one of that group, but I don't know him well.'

'Do you trust him?'

'Trust him? I don't know. Why should I need to trust him?'

'Well, you trusted me to take me to town and board a boat to find a girl.'

'Yes, but...'

'Charlie sent us after that boat. He told us that it tanked down here and that it might be where Ruby is. We know Ruby is not on the Buzzard. What if she's on Charlie's boat?'

'You are accusing Charlie of abducting Ruby?'

'Well, yes and no. I mean I don't know at all, but the Buzzard is a red herring.'

'Let's go and find Charlie.'

It starts to rain, but Chris has a big umbrella that goes over the control area and we are kept fairly dry, though there is a nippy wind. I cuddle Steven for warmth. He makes a good hot water bottle. I should be very tired by now, but I am high on adrenalin.

There isn't a fire at the Vale when we get there. The rain is too heavy for this to be a possibility, but Charlie's boat is there. Chris moors up and we make a visit to Charlie's Lazy Daze. He seems to be expecting us and has the scrumpy ready and an open packet of Rich Tea. I refuse the drink, because I need to keep my head clear.

We tell Charlie about the Canadian family and we all laugh about it. I say I want to use the facilities, which I do, but I also want to have a scout around.

Lazy Daze has a rather lazy toilet, but it is OK. I have a poke around the boat. It is shipshape with no other person on board, when I find a Molly's Cafe sugar sachet on the floor of the sleeping quarters and I know that Ruby has been on this boat. So where is she? What to do?

'Your face is familiar,' says Charlie.

'Really,' I say.

'Yes, I've seen you recently somewhere. Somewhere with the dog, I'm sure.'

'Did I have my clothes on?'

'Pardon?'

'Did I have my clothes on? Or was I in a swimming costume?'

'I don't think I should be listening to this,' says Chris.

'No, it's alright. I was swimming at The Mandalay Bay Swimming Pool and there was a wedding going on in the next room - big windows and the guests saw me. Nothing rude or lewd.'

'It was the funniest thing I've ever seen. You'd have wet yourself...'

Charlie took control of his laughter and became serious.

'You spoilt Fintan's wedding and he is going to have to pay for it, for the rest of his life.'

'Pay for as in money. Pay for as in being married to Bobby with Francine as his mother-in-law. Chris, Ruby has been on this boat.'

'Why do you say that?' Charlie is simpering.

'Because of this!' I hold up the sugar sachet.

'A little bag of sugar?'

'Yes, but not any old little bag of sugar - it's this little bag of sugar.'

'What's that? So what's that to do with anything? What are you accusing me of? I haven't done anything to be ashamed of. I want you off my boat - trouble maker.'

'Chris, he's had Ruby on this boat. She's not here now, but she has definitely been on this boat. This bag of sugar has Ruby's DNA on it.'

'DNA - you stupid woman!'

'I'm a dentist. I know about these things.'

'Get off my boat!'

Chris, Steven and I make for the All Day Breakfast.

So, Charlie is a friend of Fintan's. He had been there at the wedding and spotted me. Someone knew or spotted Ruby going into the wood and found her in the bender - maybe Francine, Beryl, angler or maybe even Charlie himself? They had arranged for Charlie to come with his boat. Or Charlie had taken the initiative to get himself there himself? He, Charlie, maybe with perhaps some others, had taken Ruby to the Vale and she had been taken off Lazy Daze from there. I think that Ruby was on Lazy Daze when I was caught by Chris on the All Day Breakfast with the tea incident.

Point of interest - I am a dentist by trade, but I know very well like most people that it is impossible to get a DNA sample from a bag of sugar that someone might have touched.

We hear Charlie cast off and go like the clappers off towards town. So where is Ruby? My guess is that she is at Francine's fortress.

'Thank you very much for your help, Chris - you have been marvelous. I'm going to get a taxi now and head home and then talk to Leslie. Oh, Leslie's Ruby's mum.'

'You can't leave me out of this. This is the most fun I have had in years. Where do you live? Where does this Francine live?'

'Francine lives in a posh house round the corner in Bastedge. Of course, Ruby is at Francine's. This is very close. Charlie takes Ruby to the Vale and then by car round the corner to Francine's house.   I'm in Knortoning. Doesn't make sense to go from here to Knortoning and then back here. I'll ring Leslie's mobile and my house phone and hopefully Leslie will answer one of them and I will try and get her to take a taxi to Francine's. Of course they all live officially with Francine - her, Leslie and Ruby. Three generations.'

'I thank God, I've no family.'

'I haven't got close family, just these cousins and their offspring. I regret not having any kids, I think. Oh I don't know. I'll try and get hold of Leslie. Leslie is a little timid. Francine's bloody-mindedness seems to have missed a generation. Ruby is a nice girl, but she is a tough one like her grandmother.'

I ring Leslie's mobile and when there's no answer I ring my home number and no one answers, so I leave a message on the answer phone telling Leslie to meet me outside Francine's house, her own home, in fact . Chris locks up the All Day Breakfast and makes sure that the ropes are well secured and we walk in silence.

Find an odd postcard in my pocket that I haven't read yet. A postcard of a Shrine, somewhere in Japan from Suz Bedgegood. It feels damp.

Hello Nancy Old Girl,

Seen very many shrines. People come up to my chest. Confirms my dislike of sushi, however jasmine tea very good. Bowing a lot. I like cats better than dogs. Sayonara, Suz xx

Yes, sayonara and off to the shrine that is Francine.

Chapter Fourteen

We get to Francine's road. The traffic is taking liberties, because it is wide, one way and a main city artery. I have forgot which house it is. In fact, is it this road? I am pretty certain that I have got the side right. As we walk past a manicured laurel hedge, Leslie jumps out of it.

'You said that Ruby was asleep in the bender. She is not in the bender at all. Not there. She is not there. I've looked. She is not there. I got your message, but what are we doing here. She is not asleep in the bender and now you have told me to come here. This is really dangerous. I don't want to be here. Ruby doesn't want to be here. I live here still because... I live here still... I live here still... I live here still, because It stops her. It stops her. Mother has me to pick on. She can pick on me. This is good. Picking on me is good. She has to leave Ruby alone. Ruby doesn't need this. I know what it is like. I know. She mustn't do it to Ruby. '

We go into the hedge with Leslie and we try to stop her from talking. She is shaking violently. Her head is moving jerkily from side to side.

'Which is the house, Leslie?'

Leslie indicates a house across the road, so I have it all wrong.

'Do you have a front door key?'

Leslie brings out a bunch of keys like a prison warder. Actually, I know that in prison, you only have a couple of keys. People think that you have a big bunch. I know lots about prison, because prisoners have teeth and often if they are users they have very bad teeth. Of course, some inmates have very well cared for teeth, because they have lots of money they shouldn't have. Fascinating places to visit as a dentist. Fascinating in any capacity as long as you don't have to spend the night there.

'I think we need a plan. The time is 11.33pm. Will the household be awake?' Chris is such a sensible man.

'She'll be up waiting for me. She'll be there and will know that I have lied. The library is not open this late. It is late night opening, but not this late. Not this late. No, not this late. It closes at 9pm. Yes, it's open until 9pm. And I haven't got a book. I haven't borrowed a book. No book. I haven't got a book, because I haven't been to the library. I've been to your house. I went to your house to say thank you and to see Ruby. I want to see Ruby. Where is Ruby? Where is Ruby? Ruby must be back home in that house.

No, she mustn't be there. No, please she mustn't be back there.'

'Let's get all this clear.' Sensible Chris.

'Right, but I must sit down soon or I'll peg out. I need and Steven needs to stop and I need to do that now. We have had a month's worth of activity in one day.'

'Is there a late night cafe or somewhere where we can talk near here, Leslie?'

'The shed. We can sit in the shed. The shed is ours. We love the shed. Follow. Follow me. She never comes to the shed. Not true. She does come to the shed, but not when it is dark. She won't be there now. Probably. Probably won't be in the shed now.'

Cars are speeding along the road from town and we take our life in our hands as Leslie and Chris run and Steven and I hobble across. The house is imposing. How can Francine afford a pile like this? Victorian? Edwardian? It breathes money.

We walk in silence except for Steven's heavy breathing and our feet on the gravel around the perimeter fence and around an Audi parked on the frontage. Leslie has her keys out and opens a side door. We walk along the side of the house and into the back garden. Chris takes out a tiny windup torch - he sure is a handy man to have about. We avoid the path and go over grass and around some trees and there is a shed. It is starting to rain again. The shed is locked with a padlock, but Leslie has the key. She opens it with Chris shining the torch on the lock. We are a team. It's years since I've felt part of a team.

The shed is lovely and it reminds me of the bender. It has the same neatness and it has obviously been well-loved. Leslie offers me the well stuffed armchair and indicates the settee to Chris that he shares with Steven. Steven likes Chris. He is always right.

Leslie brings out a large flask and pours us a hot drink each. I can't believe it, it is milk and a dash.

'Every morning, I make a flask of coffee and I bring it out here, I bring it out so that I can have a hot drink. I do my reading here. This is where Ruby and I come. This is where we come. Me and Ruby. We come here to read. We come here to be just me and Ruby. This is my home, not the house. This is where we live. This is where me and Ruby live. Like we can be us here. We can be us. Since she was a baby. Since she was a little baby. Since she was born, we have spent time here in here. This is our shed. I love our shed. It was lovely until...It was lovely until...'

'We need to know what is going on. The whole story Leslie.'

'I got pregnant at 16. This was a nasty filthy and shameful thing. Mother said I was evil. I was evil and brought shame on the family. It was shameful. So I had to live here in shame, but Ruby is not shameful.'

'Neither you nor Ruby are shameful, Leslie.'

'Now, Ruby is 16 and pregnant and mother says that this baby has to be terminated. She says terminated. Got rid off. This baby has to be flushed out of Ruby's womb, because it is a sin. A mortal sin. The baby is a mortal sin. But babies are not a sin. Babies are beautiful. Ruby has to stay away from Mother until 24 weeks is up.'

'So your mother Francine wants Ruby to have an abortion and Ruby is staying away from her until the 24 weeks are up, so she can't have an abortion. You know that it is not up to Francine. She has no rights in this. This is up to Ruby. Ruby wants the baby? Yes?'

'Oh yes, she does. Mother says that if she'd known I was pregnant that she would have got her knitting needles out. I've never understood that. She didn't know I was pregnant. I didn't know I was pregnant. I had a tummy ache one day and then I had Ruby in the school toilets. She was there. Just like that. Mother has been very good though because she has let us live here in the lap of luxury. The lap of luxury in the best part of town. We have lived here with Mother in the lap of luxury. She asks for nothing. She asks for nothing and we live in the lap of luxury.'

'I want to know why the police are not interested in Ruby living rough at 16.'

'Mother reported her missing. I took some valium and went and told them that I was her mother and that Ruby was fine and staying with her father for a bit. They believed me. I fibbed. They don't like Mother because she is always ringing them up to complain about... about.... about anything. She complains a lot. But we are very lucky to live here in the lap of luxury.I don't know much about abortions.'

'How far gone is Ruby in her pregnancy now, Leslie?'

'Not sure.'

'Ok.'

' We think that Francine got Fintan's friend Charlie to pick up Ruby from the bender and then take her on his boat Lazy Daze...'

'Yeh, I know Lazy Daze. We had a trip on it once. It's like a little shed that floats. It's lovely. That Charlie and our Fintan, they are as thick as thieves. That's what Mother says. They are as thick as thieves. So Ruby is here then. In the house. In the house with Mother. Ruby is back here. Back in the house. Back in the house with Mother. This is not good. This is not good at all. It's sad here. Mother will get Ruby to the clinic. The family will not be shamed again. That's what she says. I shamed the family and now Ruby will shame her.'

The rain is getting heavy now. It is beating on the little window.

'I think Ruby is definitely in the house. Francine, Mother, can't do much over night. Of course, you must know that she has no rights over Ruby. Ruby is not 18 yet, but you Leslie are her mum. You are the person who is legally in charge though Ruby is old enough to take some responsibility. But Francine has no rights at all.'

'Mother is getting me sectioned. That's what she says. Sectioned. What does that mean - sectioned? She will get me sectioned. She says that I have no rights. I have no rights. I am not really Ruby's mum. I was just the vessel that carried her. And I have no rights.'

'Do you believe what Mother tells you, Leslie?'

'No, no I don't. I don't believe her. She lies to me all the time. I know that, but still I believe what she says, because...'

'Because that's what she expects of you.' Says Chris.

'Yes.' Says Leslie.

Just one word answer - Leslie needs someone to be straight with her. She can and does understand.

'We need a plan for now.' Says Chris. He's very practical.

'Yes, - how about if Leslie goes in the house and let's us in. Then we'll get Ruby and then back to the All Day Breakfast.'

'All Day Breakfast - but it's night time.'

'The All day Breakfast is the name of Chris's narrowboat. Oh, by the way, Leslie, have you met my good friend Chris. Chris this is Leslie.'

'You look just like Father Christmas.'

'It has been mentioned before. It must be something to do with the beard.'

'Good plan, yes, but it means that we have to walk from here to the canal. It's a bit of a walk for you and Steven - I don't know your name either.' Chris says to me.

'I'm Nancy. Pleased to meet you.'

'I thought you were friends.' Says Leslie.

'Let's move on. Do you know where the keys to the Audi are Leslie and can you drive it?'

'Yes and no.'

' I still have my license,' I say.

'Right, Leslie will open up and the four, yes, four, don't forget Steven, will go in. Leslie will find the Audi's keys and we will find Ruby and all go back to mine. Or would you like us to drop you back at the All Day Breakfast first, Chris.'

'Back at the boat for choice.'

'Okey dokey. Let's brave the rain. After you Leslie.'

We pussy foot across the grass, but Leslie rushes back to lock the shed and then leads us to the kitchen door. She opens up and we all troop on tippy toe in the dark into this vast kitchen with a red Aga. It is lit up like a ocean going liner. A red Aga that obviously has never been used. It is magnificent and very warm even from a distance. I fall instantly in love and go and embrace it.

'I'd love an Aga. I'd love a red Aga.'

'Ssssshhhhhhhh!' says Chris.

We drip a muddy path across the kitchen floor.   The others join me for a warm.

'This kettle is boiling anyone fancy another drink?' I say.

'Yes, please,' they say and with that the light goes on.

Francine stands in her nighty in the doorway, holding a meat cleaver. She looks a bit cross.

'Intruders! So this is how you repay me, Leslie Gloria Frederica Byrde. This is how you repay the years that I have given you and your bastard a home. You bring the lowest of the low into this house in the middle of the night. There is only one thing for it!'

Francine flicks a switch on the wall activates an alarm with flashing lights . The whole house is consumed by noise and lights.

This is too much for Steven. I think he was trying to bite into Francine's jugular, but he seemed to get hold of something up inside her nighty. She screams blue murder and, in fact, Steven lets go very fast. He doesn't want a bite/suck whatever it he has. While this is going on, Chris walks past Francine into the body of the house. She doesn't seem to see him.

'We have come for Ruby.' Says Leslie.

I can't believe it. She is direct and firm - fantastic!

'You are not fit to be a mother.' Screams Francine.

Chris comes back into the kitchen and shouts to us to get outside.

We all follow him out to the front of the house, including Francine. And there is Ruby on the low roof of the conservatory. Her door has been locked by Granfran from the outside, so she had got out onto the roof through the window. The Audi is parked close to the wall and without a second thought, Chris gets onto the back bumper, then the boot and then the roof. He helps Ruby onto the car and then down the same way.

Ruby is in her jamas. She runs to her mother.

'This is abduction - the police! Fintan! Charlie! Is Charlie still here?' Francine runs back in the house.

'The keys?'

To my amazement, Leslie has the keys. I can't open the doors, but Ruby does it. Leslie, Steven and Chris get in the back. I get in the driver's seat and Ruby climbs over me to sit in the front passenger seat. I put the key in the ignition and reverse when I hoped to go forward.

'Swop,' says Ruby to me. I get out. Ruby climbs into the driver's seat and moves the car so that I can get in the passenger seat. Ruby put her foot down and careers into the heavy traffic. There is honking of horns. Ruby drives to my house with her foot on the accelerator. Not bad for a 16 year old without a lesson or a license.

We get back to mine, Steven asleep in my arms and it is very late. Somehow we forgot to take Chris back to the All Day Breakfast. Maybe Ruby didn't know this was a plan.

'We can't leave the Audi here. Parked here, people will know that is was us who took it.' I say.

'Granfran was in the house when we drove away, so she knows we have it.' Says Ruby.

'I have an idea. Give me the keys, Ruby. I'll see you all tomorrow. It will be early morning. I'll bring the boat down here and moor up outside if that's OK Nancy?' Chris says and leaves us.

I put Ruby and Leslie in the spare bedroom. There was no talk of going to the bender - thank God. It was still peeing down with rain. I decide I'll sit up and wait for Chris. Steven's snores send me off as I sit in my chair.

I'm woken up by the sound of a boat outside. I must have been asleep longer than I thought. So I go and put the kettle on and go outside to catch the rope and help moor up. But to my horror. It is not the All Day Breakfast. It's Lazy Daze with Charlie at the helm and even worse, out of the cabin, comes Fintan.

'This mooring is reserved,' I say - is this the best I can do?

'Out of the way - I've come for them.' Fintan pushes me aside and strides up the footpath.

Sadly, Steven is fast asleep. His suck is worse than his bite.

'How dare you young man? I am here alone. Don't you dare enter - they are up at the bender.'

'The bender? Homosexual?' Fintan seems puzzled.

'The little camp up in the woods. You know where it is, I'm sure, you do.'

Fintan stops in his tracks.

'That makes sense, Fintan.We'd better take Lazy Daze. So we can take them on the boat up to the Vale for transfer to the house.'

'Yeh, OK. I'd rather do it in the light, but... beggars can't be choosers.'

'We'll have to turn round. There's a winding point just ahead before the Wast Hill Tunnel.'

I curse the fact I haven't got Chris's mobile number. I don't know in fact if he has a mobile, but most boaters do, in case of a breakdown.

I have to think carefully. The Lazy Daze is going South down the canal and so will Chris in the All Day Breakfast, but when Lazy Daze turns around they will be heading towards each other. This is not good. I think a confrontation is not a good idea, if it can be avoided, particularly in the dark. I don't know exactly where Chris is, but I know that he is heading towards the All Day Breakfast at the Vale. So I ring for a taxi.

'I know it's in the middle of the night and I am fully aware that it will cost me an arm and a leg. I want a taxi asap or sooner. Careful, or I'll take my custom elsewhere.'

Khaver Khan is doing a night shift and he is most helpful and he's sad that Steven is not with me. I have left Steven at home and the two women asleep, but I leave a note saying that I'll be back in a bit.

I'm dropped at the Vale and I see that the car is parked there and that Chris is on board the boat as the lights are on.

I tell Chris about Fintan and Chris and we work out a cunning plan. Chris has Charlie's mobile number and sends a text.

Les & Rube with me at Vale. C U

He turns his mobile phone off. He doesn't want to get into a dialogue - very wise.

Then we get in motion. I steer the All Day Breakfast to just below Bourneville Train Station. Bournville Train Station is on the towpath. Steering is quite a task for me. I have never been in charge of a boat before, let alone a boat in the dark. I have to move quickly too. It has good lights so that is great. I might be able to see what I'm crashing into. I have to remember - move the stick to the left, if I want to go right and turn the stick to the right, if I want to go left. Chris takes the Audi to the roadway there. He'll get there before me, so he'll park the Audi across the roadway with a front bumper parallel to the edge of the canal. He'll then walk along towards me and jump on the All Day Breakfast as soon as we meet.

For a first effort, all things considered, I don't do a bad job, considering I am in a 71ft boat in the dark. It's not too bad, really it's not - no proper lesson at all.

I spot Chris at Selly Oak and I manage to get close enough to the bank for him to pop on.
He takes over. And we really increase speed until we get just past the Audi. We moor briefly. Chris gets off the boat taking the boat hook with him. The boat hook is in two parts and he unscrews them so he has two poles, one with a hook on the end. He gets in the car, opens all the windows and fires up the engine. Then he gets out of the car and with great ingenuity, he pressed down on the accelerator pedal with one pole and with the hook end he slips the handbrake.

The Audi makes a spectacular dive into the canal and slowly sinks.

Chris boards the All Day Breakfast again and we move to the other side of the bridge and moor under the branches of some trees on the opposite side. Without the lights on, we are quite well camouflaged. This is where the towpath changes sides, so we can get off the boat, walk up to the bridge and over the road. From this vantage point, we can see what is happening around the car that is now under water.   Chris puts his mobile phone back on and it makes some twitting sounds, but he rubs the messages off without reading them and puts it into video mode. The light won't be good, but...

Lazy Daze rockets underneath us, lights ablazing and it hits the submerged Audi with a terrific crash and whoop of water spray, explodes into the air. The engine dies. We can hear the blaspheming clearly.   Chris has it on video. It's very poor quality, but...

We move off slowly back to my house and Chris moors up. Steven, Leslie and Ruby are still asleep.

There is a postcard sticking out of the letter box.

Postcard of scary Peking Opera Actor, Beijing from Suz Bedgegood

Hello Nancy Old Girl,

Saw demonstration of Peking Opera make-up - quite interesting if you are going out for a night out. The Food is not like our lovely Wok 'n' Go in town. You can eat duck's webs here if you must. I was your best friend before the dog.

Zai jian, Suz xx

Ah, yes, a night out. This has been a night out, Suz.

Chapter Fifteen

So, it's morning, Steven and I are awake. Chris is outside on the All Day Breakfast. I presume that Leslie and Ruby are still asleep. I need a pee and because it is just me usually, the lock system on the bathroom is not good. So I push the door open and Leslie is at the sink. There are a full top and bottom set of false teeth on the side of the sink.

And the penny drops.

The teeth are expensively made, very good quality teeth. I have been hoodwinked into thinking they are Leslie's real teeth. The ones she was born with.

My life in teeth and dental care has been full and I like to think successful. In my experience, very serious tooth decay can be caused by many things, but often it is drug related. Cocaine or as its called by users, Crack, is often rubbed onto the teeth and gums. This takes off the enamel of the tooth and buggers the gums. Heroin is rough on teeth, because it and other drugs too cause sugar cravings. This will, together with the dental neglect that often comes with substance abuse, will cause serious damage.

There have been lots of bad teeth lately - the angler, Fintan and now Leslie. Does Charlie have trouble with his molars? He's got a thick beard that takes your attention? Chris has a beard - ??? Must check. Someone else, I've seen recently had bad teeth -???

I back out of the bathroom and go to the All Day Breakfast to check Chris's teeth. Surprisingly, I am quite subtle.

'Do you have false teeth, Chris?'

Well, it's better than putting a hand in his mouth.

He doesn't and his pearlies are all his own. This is good news.

I invite Chris in for a bacon sandwich. I don't want to put him off, by suggesting kippers. Ruby is sitting at the table and I must admit, I have a very good look at her teeth. They look fine. I tell her that she should take advantage of the free dental care for pregnant mothers and she tells me that she knows all about it and goes regularly to Pearl White, the nice dentist close to Francine's.

As Ruby looks starving the cooking of breakfast becomes a big meal with not just bacon, but sausage, tomatoes, black pudding, fried eggs and mushrooms and loads of toast. We are all ravenous. Steven eats a packet of rubber bacon. We all eat, because we don't want to talk plans, because no one has any ideas, I think. Chris and I don't tell anyone about the Audi incident. Better to keep that to ourselves.

The other thing is that drugs are dangerous. The people who sell them are dangerous. I don't think that Leslie and Ruby are at all, but... we have to be very careful. Can I trust them? Do I need to trust them? What am I becoming part of? I think I have to be very careful indeed.

We, that's all five of us, decide that we'll all go up to the bender. Chris wants to see it, he has good memories of Greenham Common, his sister was there and he used to deliver her Jack Daniels.

Geoff the angler is there at his spot on the other side of the canal. Leslie stops and looks across to him. He takes no notice of any of us. When we get to the bender, it is a sorry sight. It was left open when Fintan and Charlie took Ruby away and it had rained steadily all night. The sleeping bag and her My Little Pony pillow are completely sodden. We take the bedding back to the house for a hot wash.

When we got back to the house, Chris goes off up the Stratford Canal to Lyon's Boatyard to keep the All Day Breakfast out of harms way and around other people. He said he'll get the number 18 bus back as soon as he can. I sit the girls down. It's time for some straight talking.

'First of all, I don't think you have anywhere obvious where you can stay. I mean, I don't think there is a building with a roof, hot and cold running, a toilet, heating and a kitchen where you can stay. I think that if you had options, Ruby would not have been living like a hedgehog in a pile of leaves, even if it was a nice cosy pile of leaves. I know things are very difficult and we should talk about all that, but in the short term you need somewhere to stay and I would like to offer you my spare bedroom. You would have to put up with me and a toothless smelly dog with a gammy leg, but we are not too bad if you are desperate and I think you are.'

They nod their heads in unison.

'I feel safe here.' says Leslie

'It seems that both of you have done things that you haven't wanted to. I am not forcing you to say yes. It's up to you and the room is there. It is an offer. OK?' I say.

I carry on 'Does Ruby know about your drug addiction Leslie?'

'Yes, I do and it makes a nonsense of the stuff we're taught at school. Yeh, Tobacco is bad, but what about all the other stuff and it's not just the illegal stuff, alcohol is bloody destructive too.' Ruby jumps in.

'I am not an alcoholic.'

'I know Mum. I know you're not. Oh don't worry, Nance, I know all about all of it.'

'You know most, Ruby. Where shall I start?'

"You know I'm a dentist, Leslie. Well, I was a dentist. And we both know that illegal drugs can really bugger your teeth. So when did you start using and what is your.... mmmm.....
drug of choice?' She didn't answer me.

'OK? So how did it all start then?'

'He said it would make me feel better. He said that I was a bit down, a bit depressed and maybe it was post natal depression. Women do get to feeling a bit down, you know, after they have had a baby. I felt down after I had Ruby. It

123

wasn't that I wasn't happy to have Ruby. No. Ruby is the best thing that has ever happened to me. I love Ruby. I love being a mum. I wish I was a good mum. I'm a lousey mum. I wish I was a good mum. My Ruby deserves a good mum, not one like me. I am not a good mum. Mother said I didn't deserve to be a mother. Did I tell you that she told me that. Did I tell you that she told me that before. Anyway, he said it would make me feel better. He said I needed cheering up and that it would cheer me up. Yes, that's what I needed I needed cheering up. It would cheer me up. He gave me tablets at first. Tablets that looked like paracetamol. Pills. Happy pills. They made me happy. Later things came in different shapes and stuff. Colours even, but the first ones looked like headache pills. You know for a headache.'

'Where was this then, Leslie?'

'At home, of course.'

'You mean in that big old house in Bastedge.? Francine's big old house? The one you've always lived in?'

'I was scared of needles. Well, you are, aren't you? Scared of them. They hurt, don't they? I was scared of the needle the first time. A girl at school used to prick her finger with a jabby thing to test, to test her blood, I think. Then she had a big needle and she would inject herself. Not the school nurse. Oh no, she'd do it herself. The needle and all the stuff would be in Miss's cupboard with all the books - under lock and key. Kept safe. No, not the books, I mean, but the needle and the stuff. It was Ok, because no one, no, no one wanted to have a needle stuck in their arm. Anyway, she would inject herself. He said it would make me feel

124

better. He said it was just like Shirley's needle. That it was medicine, like Shirley's. It would make me feel better.   I didn't want him to do it. He said I needed it. He said I needed it and that Mother said I needed something. Anyway, I gave him my arm and he stabbed me, but then I could feel this stuff, this medicine going into my body. This warmth trickling into my body. I lay down, I think. I think...can't remember...can't remember, but soon I was warm and happy. I had never felt so...so...I don't know. I don't know the word. It was just...and then later..it went... it went... the medicine? I needed more. I needed more...he gave me more. He gave me more for ...for...for...for years.'

'Who was it, Leslie? Who gave you whatever it was?'

'Fintan, of course.'

'So your sister's boyfriend. I suppose your brother-in-law now. He gave you some sort of illegal substance in your own home?'

'Yes.'

'Of course he has a habit too. You know that?' Ruby says.

'No, he hasn't. Bobby says it's controlled.'

'Oh she does, does she?'

'Yes.'

'So Fintan gave you something to make you happy in your own home.'

'Yes, but it was alright, because Mother knew all about it.'

'Francine! Francine knew that you were given drugs by that bastard Fintan!'

'That's a strong word, Nancy, the b word.'

'No, it's not Mum. He's a shit!' Ruby broke in.

And with that, there was banging on the door.

Chapter Sixteen

I will not open the door to thugs. I go upstairs and look out the window. Fintan is standing on the path. Along the fence is a menacing line of men with bald heads and one hairy one - Charlie.

'Hello, can I help you?'

'You know what we want. But now it's not just the two of them, it's you too. Get your things together all of you. You will be sometime.'

I am like a jelly.

'I'm the only person here. I s'ppose you are talking about that nice young woman, oh and yes, your sister-in-law. Did the mother-in-law send you on an errand?' I laugh and the bald men laugh too.

'Hello boys! Good to see you. Are you being paid much for coming down the towpath then? Or are you doing it out of the kindness of your hearts? Or are you being paid with a bit of wacky baccy or something to shove up your nose.'

They look a bit like a class of naughty infants.

' I think I recognise some of you.' Which I don't. ' School dentist. Gaz with the cavities. Baz with an extraction lots of gas and is that John with a wisdom tooth that came too early. Got the tooth, but not the wisdom. Yes?'

They all look from one to each other.

The shortest shouts up 'Sorry to bother you, Miss.'

They shuffle off towards the road as good as gold. I was only a school dentist for an afternoon, but it seemed to work. Charlie looking sheepish followed them.

Fintan looks naked, though of course, he is fully clothed in tracky bottoms and a tee shirt that reads *You look like I need another beer.*

' Francine will hear about this. I'll be back you bitch from hell with real re-enforcements next time.' Fintan shouts and jumps up and down at the same time.

That all seems too easy, but no mention of Lazy Daze . All too easy.

I go downstairs and Leslie and Ruby are shivering on the sofa. I could be a little bit fed up with their lack of support for something that is really their problem. But of course, it is not just their problem. I s'ppose there are men who have been terrorised by women, but it is usually, men who abuse women. But then I have a brief think and the person who is deadly in this situation is Francine. I think that Francine is like a Mafia boss, sort of Don Coleone in a twin set. Where did she get the money from for that house? Was she really married to a colonel who fathered her children? As her cousin, I should know these things, but I was having a good time in Edinburgh at Dental School when all the procreating was going on.

Now what?

First any post? A brochure for the new season at Symphony Hall, a voucher for dog toothpaste (no good for a dog without teeth) and a postcard of a paddy field, I think.

Hello Nancy Old Girl,

Lots of rice here too. Weather quite pleasant really for those of us used to travel. They tried to get me on a bicylce. Had second thought about taking the train through to Bangkok. Will take a nice plane instead. Lots of dogs here - all very skinny.

Xin chào, Suz xx

She can't spell *BICYCLE*. Chris could do with a bike. Does he have one?

Second thing?

Chris? Where is Chris? I'll ring. I ring. Answer phone. I leave a message to ring.

My phone goes. It's Chris.

'Hello Petal, Yeh, I'm up at the boatyard getting some diesel. Yes. I've got a bit of news. There is a panic on here.'

He's talking very loudly.

'You know Charlie the bloke with Lazy Daze - well, he drove into a car. The car, wait for it, was in, yes, in the canal. Someone had driven it, into the canal. It was in the water and Charlie poor bloke drove the boat into it. People from here have gone up to see it and then to bring the boat back to the yard for repairs. It's a heavy old tub, but the nose is crumpled I understand and there's damage to the engine too.... The car? Don't know, but someone said that the police are organising a crane. The divers have been out already and there are no bodies inside. So they don't think it's a suicide attempt anymore. It seems it's an Audi. Well, it was an Audi. What a terrible waste. Yeh, I'll pop over in a bit. On my bike OK? See yers.'

I suspect that the call came from the chandlery shop full of people. Well done, Chris.And he does have a bicycle.

Leslie and Ruby are back in bed. Shivering and it isn't cold. So I take up three cups of tea and Steven for extra warmth as a hot water bottle.

'Let's take it from the beginning, Leslie. Try and tell it from the beginning.'

'Well, as you know Nancy, you know the family and everything. Well, I was born to Francine sometime after Bobby. You know all about that. How much difference is There? Don't know? Almost 2 years. 2 years? Yeh, about 2 years.'

'I never quite understood about your father Leslie.'

'Army Nancy. He was in the army. Yes, the army. A colonel in the army. He was a colonel. In the army, yes, that's right.'

'Do you remember him then Leslie?'

'Not really, no, but he was in the army. He was a colonel. In the army.'

'And you've always lived in the house in Bastedge, haven't you?'

'Yes, that's right. That's right, isn't it, Ruby?'

' Now you had Ruby when you were 16 years old, didn't you, Leslie?'

'That's right. I had to leave school.'

'Was Francine pleased?'

'She was furious. Mother was furious.'

'Who is Ruby's father, Leslie?'

'She doesn't know you silly old cow. She doesn't know who he was. Don't you think I'd know, if she knew. She doesn't know.' Ruby is instantly upset with me and not her Mum.

'Usually, women have some sort of idea of who the father of their children is. I know that sometimes it could be any number of men and I know sometimes a pregnancy comes out of a traumatic experience.'

Silence.

'Let's leave that for now. Let's jump to now. Why are you living secretly in a bender in the woods?' I ask Ruby.

'Hiding seems to be the only option. Granfran wants, no, demands that I have an abortion. She doesn't want me to have a baby like mum did at 16. She has found it difficult to live with the shame last time. Oh yes, and you realise that the shame is me. I am the shame. It's me. She, that's Granfran, has organised a trip for me to go to a clinic. She has been quite honest. She said that if she had any idea that Mum was pregnant with me that she would have taken Mum to that place. Mum didn't realise she was pregnant and neither did Granfran so I was allowed to live. My baby is going to be allowed to live too. I want my baby very much. I am not. I repeat will not have my baby aborted, terminated, killed. '

' Mother taught Bobby and I to make a bender when we were little. She was at Greenham for a very short time, so making a bender seemed a good idea. I come down to Ruby when I could with supplies and Geoff does too. Mother called the police, but I told them that Ruby was staying with friends.They believed me rather than Mother, because she rings them all the time about nothing.'

'It's funny that Granfran phones the police all the time and that she is the head of a drugs ring.' Says Ruby.

'So she is?' I say.

'Oh yes, she supplies most of town with their illegal substances.'

'So Francine sells drugs...'

'Not directly to the customer. Fintan does that. He does very well, because he has a bad habit. But the house is the depot where everything is delivered to and then taken from. It's like Tescos, in and out. Charlie brings lots of stuff in from Bristol and delivers stuff all around the West Midlands as well. No one suspects things, because Granfran is such a pillar of the community and she is ringing the police all the time.' Ruby adds.

'So it's Francine as mastermind, Fintan as general manager, Charlie logistics and who travels abroad and things to get the stuff here?'

As we are just getting to the interesting bit. The door bell goes. Steven goes to the door and wags his tail, so I know it is a friend, not a foe. It's Chris on his bicycle.

'Come on ladies - time for brunch up at Mollies. It's on me.'

'Good idea, Steven could do with a walk.'

'Can we go via the bender, please? I'd like to pick up some more things maybe.' Asks Ruby.

So off we trot.

No Geoff the angler there today and the moss is starting to cover the bench. You can just see the blue words faintly.

The bender is gone. There are no signs of it all. It is as if it has never been there. It's difficult to work out where it was. But someone has been there and removed any sign of it. This must have been particularly difficult as it was made of natural things from the wood and then adorned by litter. Ruby is upset, because in many ways it was her safe place.

We walk up the village in silence. Even Steven is quite subdued until he realises that we are going to Mollies. He is given a wonderful welcome and a free sausage. We all squeeze around a small table. It is always busy in Mollies. Chris orders five full English. What Steven doesn't eat of his, Ruby will.

The window looks out onto the Green and as we are waiting, I spot someone sitting on a bench, head in hands. He looks vaguely familiar and then I realise that it is Charlie. He must have come up to the Green after the show of strength (not) on the towpath. None of us is saying much after the shock of the bender site, so we are sort of playing a game of chess with no rules with salt, pepper and various sauce bottles.

For something to say, I say 'look there's Charlie.'

And Chris stands up and walks out of Mollies toward Charlie on the bench.I look at the crispy bacon and with regret I feel I should follow. Steven with another sausage in his mouth comes too.

'Hello Charlie, will I see you later in the week at the Vale for a jar?'

'Don't think so matey. The boat is in dock at Lyon's. Had a bit of a bump. It takes ages for repairs and the poor old Lazy Daze will have to come out of the water to get a full view of the damage.'

'I'm moored up at Lyon's at the moment. Nice people. Fair price. There was talk of a collision. A car or something. I couldn't believe it.'

"Yeh, collision with an Audi. Someone had driven an Audi into the canal.'

'That takes some getting your head around.'

Then Charlie sees that I am standing behind Chris.

'What are you doing with that old bat? Bloody Madam Fang.' Says Charlie.

Chris laughs. Unkindly, I think.

'Hello, Charlie. It's good to see you on your own. Do you want to join us for breakfast. We are over at Mollies. We've got some friends with us. I think you know Leslie and Ruby. In fact I think Ruby had a little trip on your boat. They have just popped over on the number 11 bus to Kings Heath and then the 18. They are staying in a safe house in Erdington. Oh shit, I shouldn't have said that.'

I try to be crafty. I think that Charlie is not the sharpest knife in the drawer.

'Not with you then?' says Charlie.

Chris and I laugh.

'Of course not. That would be a bit silly, wouldn't? Too close to home. No, they are safe in Erdington, I don't know exactly. I think it's over the Witton side - you know - where there's that enormous graveyard that overlooks the M6. Rest in peace in a traffic jam.'

I'm getting carried away now. Time to shut up. It's time for me to get back to my breakfast. Steven gives Charlie a warning growl and follows me. He wants another sausage. Chris stays and has a final word.

When we are back to Mollies, the women have shifted most of their food. We three dive in. It's just hot enough, but the butter doesn't melt into the toast. I ask for another couple of rounds, while eating the cold stuff anyway.

'Tell us what happened, when Charlie and Fintan took you on the Lazy Daze up to Bastedge, Ruby.'

'Well, I was talking to you wasn't I? On my phone. Didn't hear anyone coming, which is strange. I heard the boat, I think, but you always hear boats, don't you? Anyway, we are talking and then the side opens suddenly and Charlie and Fintan are in. It took a second to know what was happening. I think I had been expecting it. When they threw me in the boat, Granfran was there waiting for me.'

'On board?'

'Oh yes, and she started giving me a lecture about loyalty to the family and the family business. At that I was being groomed to take over and that's why she was paying for me to have an expensive education. I was an investment. She wants this new bastard on the block removed. That's what she said - after you have this new bastard removed.'

'She is wicked. I know we are cousins and I knew she was not a good person, but such wickedness...'

'It's all my fault. Mine. I should have... I could have... I needed to be strong. I needed to be stronger. I should have got away. Me and Ruby should have got away. I have tried to be a good mum to Ruby, but it is hard when your own mother is so ...is so...is so....'

'I'm making no complaints Mum. I love you, but you are right. You should have left when I was a baby.'

'I told Charlie you are staying in a safe house - whatever that is. I think it sort of implies that the police are involved and actually they need to be, but we'll talk about this when we get home. I've told him that you are staying in Erdington, the Witton end by the graveyard. Now that won't hold for long, but he'll feed that back to Fintan and from him to Francine and it will give us a bit of breathing space. Everyone finished their brekkie? Yes, well, let's get back to the house. Chris, if you go and have a quick word with Charlie while we go down to the bus stop. Oh, no need, he's gone. Mmmmmm, I think I'd rather know where he is, I think.'

We walk back cautiously. Watching people. We bump into Rolo the dachshund with his owner Jolly Face going for walk and I'm asked if I know about the car in the canal and I say no I don't. How interesting. Then there's Daisy and `Penny the greyhounds with Greyhound Joan. Again, had I heard about the car in the canal? And she knew even more - she knew that a boat had driven into it. It was a boat that comes up and down our bit of the Cesterrow and Hammingbrum all the time.

Yes, This boat is not a leisure boat. Charlie doesn't move up and down from Bristol to Hammingbrum because it is a lovely trip and that the Severn is a particularly wonderful river to travel on. No. The Lazy Daze is, in fact, a commercial boat. It is a working boat. Though it's cargo may be illegal. It is, in fact, carrying merchandise between two great cities, the last leg of an international journey.

There are so many things to find out and 'course, it needs to stop.

As we walk down to the towpath, the smell of something very herbal floats up from under the bridge. I walk down there and there are five spotty youths passing around a spliff. I know what a spliff is - I was a teenager in the 60's.

'It addles your brains, boys.'
Five boys are showing their designer underpants.

'You will become grey. It will sap your energy and enthusiasm for life. Ruby - do you find any of these young man sexually attractive? '

"No way, Nancy. Their eyes are funny and they smell like shit.' Says Ruby.

'I bet you think you are sexually potent, don't you boys? They think they are chilled out Ruby. Slowing down? Yes. Lightheaded? Yes. It will effect the way you behave, think and feel. They are relaxed and happy, Ruby. He's giggling a lot - something is funny and he wants to interrupt us. He is feeling very talkative. Yeh, have another drag - move onto being faint and sick. On yes, then it's welcome anxiety, panic and paranoia. You will after time become the grey men.'

We walk along the towpath away from them and towards the house.

'Load of virgins.' Shouts Ruby over her shoulder and back at them.

On the towpath, the ducks are out in full strength. Ruby and I admire them and compare our names for them. Derek is Rio in Rubyland, Michael is Tarquin, the twins Barry and Harry are Mark and Spencer. Poppy is Skye and Geraldine is Hyacinth. There is a girl called Hyacinth in Ruby's class at school who walks like a duck. There is a new duck on the block too and we call her Francine because of her big beak. She is a comedy duck that continuously quacks.

This makes me also think about Ruby and school - she should be attending. Another thing to put on the list of things to remember to talk about.

It's sunny and the canal is like Piccadilly Circus. Carpe Diem is coming up north, followed by Barn Owl. Coming south is Buzzard with its Canadian crew still belting along. They see Chris and me and mime shooting us with grins on their faces. We pretend to fall over and die. Leslie doesn't think it is funny and starts to shake. Ruby gives her a hug and winks at me.

So we get back to the house without any new incidents. Time to talk and maybe it's time to make another pot of tea. As I am host and unwittingly the leader of the pack, I get my enormous drawing pad and felt tips out, so that we can put things down and try to take control. Francine has taken control, now it's our turn.

I go into the conservatory with my big pad of paper and felt pens to make a plan. A big plan so that everyone can offer ideas and so we can put the plan up on the wall with drawing pins, so we can all see it. I love stationery. I love Staples the shop. The others are following and sitting there is Francine - talk of the devil.

'How the hell did you get into my house? Get out now! Have you got your hatchet man with you?'

Francine is a very funny colour and breathing heavily. Her eyes seem unfocused and weird. She is clutching her...

The others come in.

Francine vomits all over the table. Oh my God!

Ruby jumps into action.

'Granfran - your tablets. Where are your tablets?'

Francine shakes her head wildly.

Ruby gets her mobile and rings 999. It's for an ambulance and I'm very impressed that Ruby gives very clear directions to find the house without a road and on the canal, but it still takes the ambulance people thirty minutes to get to the house. They have to fight through any number of Canal and River Trust volunteers who are cleaning up the walkway down to the canal and painting over graffiti on the signage.Bet the spotty youths moved on quickly, when they saw their yellow waistcoats.

The ambulance man Curtis, that's what his badge says, wants someone to go with Francine in the ambulance, but neither Leslie nor Ruby will go. The abuse runs so deep, even though Ruby rang for help, neither her nor her mum will go to the hospital with her. Ruby sends Bobby a text and then turns her phone off.

How did Francine get into the house? Who was she expecting to see? Probably just me I think. She will have heard that Ruby and Leslie are living in a safe house in Erdington. Come on Nancy, Charlie might be stupid, But Francine isn't. She knows that Rubes and Les are living here.

The emergency key? The emergency key under the mat? It's not there. Francine has it. She comes to the house. Looks under the mat. Finds the emergency key - comes in to wait for me and has a heart attack. She is now traveling to A & E with the emergency key. At hospital she will see Bobby who is married to Fintan and sooner or later that key will get to Fintan. Having said that Fintan could and would easily put a brick through a window, not having a front door key would not stop Fintan. He would prefer to break in and enter.

I think about all these things as I take Steven for a little walk up to the second bench and back. The volunteers must use some special cleaner. They have attacked the bench and there is no trace of the offending words. This is good. Geoff the angler is not there, neither is the little tent. I think that if Ruby is not in residence then he is not needed. Needed in any capacity.

I get back home. I have questions, that need answers.

'They have cleaned the words off the second bench.'

'Who has?' Says Ruby.

'Those volunteers. There are loads of them. They are wearing those florescent yellow waistcoats, just in case you can't see them.'

'Right.'

'Ruby, did you write the words 'fuck bench' on that bench in blue paint? It doesn't matter if you did. I'd just like to know. Did you?'

'No, I didn't. If I was painting graffiti on that bench, I would have written 'the conception bench' on it.'

'Oh, right, I see. Do you know who did write on it?'

The question hangs in the air and Ruby goes to put the kettle on.

We drink tea.

I check the letter box. there's a postcard. It's of boats on a river. Bangkok? Thailand?

Hello Nancy Old Girl,

Lovely hotel with all the trimmings. Lots of smiling staff. Food good if you like their green and red curries, which I don't. It's great place to diet.

Pai - kwan, Suz xx

I put it with the others, in the downstair's loo.

Chapter Seventeen

The five of us sit at the table. Chris looks very comfortable in my father's old chair. Ruby and Leslie are on the bench and I'm on the high back chair. My leg is giving me gip. We drink tea and it is time to get to the bottom of whatever is going on.I keep on thinking that, but have a suspicion that I will never know all the answers.

'Why did Francine tell me to keep the 27th free for Bobby and Fintan's wedding and then not invite me?'

'That's easy,' says Leslie,'she knew if she invited you, that you wouldn't come to it. By telling you to keep it free and then not inviting you, she guaranteed that you would be out of the house. She wanted you out of the house, Nancy. She wanted you and Steven away.'

'She didn't know that you would turn up in the pool in your cossie and upstage the whole do.' Ruby giggles and then Ruby turns serious.

'I was supposed to be a bridesmaid and I had refused. Granfran was angry that I had refused, but she didn't want me there either, because I was beginning to show. And, let's be frank, after she had had a 16 old pregnant daughter , she didn't want to show off a 16 year old pregnant granddaughter 16 years later. They all knew I would be where ever I was. Charlie on the Lazy Daze had spotted Geoff fishing. He'd noticed that Geoff always seemed to be there at that particular spot. So Francine on the day that everyone would be at the Mandalay Bay, sent the dogs in.'

'Sent the dogs in?"

'Yeh, the dogs. Fintan has contacts with dogs with teeth. I heard that he gave them my old rabbit Mr Rabbit to sniff and they were going to flush me out. But these dogs are just very nasty, not trained to find anyone. They rushed about in the wood barking and yapping. They didn't find me, but they found the take away curry that Geoff had brought down that I left by the bench.I was going to eat , but I was very sick that day. Geoff and I watched from the other side of the canal. I think I saw you and Steven later. I left the 'thank you' note to you too.'

'They wanted to find you. So they wanted me out of the way, because I'm nosey and there is Steven here who might take on the dogs and win. And they wanted an alibi, in case something went wrong with the flushing out with dogs and what better alibi than everyone at a wedding. Even me. Francine knows me better than I thought. And you watched the dogs, because you were with Geoff under lots of layers. I saw you cooking bacon when I came back. We smelt it, didn't we Steven.'

Chris looked confused.

'So you invite someone verbally and then withdraw the invitation and then you know they will come. Nancy, you have a very weird family.'

'Not close family. I have no close family.'

Leslie turned to me and says 'I think we are now.'

I ignore this, though, in my heart of hearts, I do hope she's right.

'So, let's get a few things straight - Geoff the angler?'

'Geoff the fake angler.'

'OK, Geoff the faker angler - good guy or bad guy?'

'Both, more good now.'

'Yes,' confirms Leslie.

'He used to be a user, now he just smokes a little weed to relax...'

'Oh yes,' I jump in. 'I know what we mean - relax!'

'He has MS now.' Leslie puts her head to one side to show sympathy.

'Yes,' says Ruby ' but he used to do everything and he was Granfran's most successful salesperson. He sold lots and it fed his habit.'

'Habits.' Chipped in Leslie.

'He doesn't sell anymore, because he's slowed down a bit. Fintan just passes on a bit of grass for old times sake.'

'That's very good of him.' From Chris.

' He will probably take up fishing properly' Leslie says.

'So I know that the drugs - whatever they are, are brought up from Bristol by Charlie in Lazy Daze. Then they go the very short distance to Francine's house and stored there for distribution and Fintan heads that operation. Right?'

'Yes that's right.'

'And Francine is overprotective or has bullied you, Leslie, in staying with her, because she wants control of you and your daughter, Ruby. She's grooming Ruby to take over the business. Don't suppose Fintan is happy with that. He's got four kids to follow him. Both he and Francine have no scruples at all about illegal drugs, have they? No. So now for an interesting question - how did this all start and who is running the foreign connection? Illegal drugs don't just turn up in Bristol there for the taking, do they?'

'It's the Colonel.' Leslie says.

'The Colonel, Your dad? I've always presumed he was your dad and Bobby's. And if he's your dad, Leslie, then he's Ruby's grandfather? The Colonel - Francine's long lost husband?'

'Yeh, he travels around. He can't get back into the UK, even though he's still married to Granfran. He's a US citizen of course and he's been inside for long stints but that's ok, because no one here wants to see him. He could pay to get back in here, but there really is no reason - the UK side of the business ticks over nicely and he's too busy jetsetting to bother to come to Brum. He just looks after the acquisition side - you know Colombia, Mexico, Thailand and the manufacturing in the US. It's shipment to Nigeria and then from there to Bristol. Francine and Fintan are not interested in that, they just want local and a share in the profits.' Says Ruby truthfully.

'How on earth did all this come about? I mean Francine and Beryl had a wholesome upbringing, I s'ppose a bit like mine. Of course, they both went to boarding school and I didn't. They say that boarding school warps your belief systems. I think they were shipped out when they were very little - probably about 7 ish. We were a little surprised that Francine married the Colonel. Not many women, I s'pect married American soldiers when they went to Greenham Common to protest against Cruise Missiles. Both sides were kept pretty separate, I think. I thought he hung around long enough to inseminate Francine twice and then buggered off.'

'That is truly gross, Nancy. You shouldn't talk like that with me here. I am only 16.'

'Yes and old enough to be pregnant, young woman.'

'So how did the Colonel get involved with drugs.' Chris asks.

'Long story. I'll tell it mum. You've told me about it often enough. We'll go all around the houses and be up half the night, if you do it. Is that Ok?'

'Let's sit in the front room on the comfy chairs. I think this is going to be a long story. Bring the teapot.There's some prawn vol-au-vents that we can nibble on too.'

And Ruby told us the whole story of the Cadaver Connection.

'This is the story according to Granfran. This is the story that the Colonel told her and this is the story that she told Mum. It may not be true.

It all started in Vietnam - you know the Vietnam War. The Colonel was a private when he served in Vietnam. He was 18. He was drafted and at that time, many who were sent drafted papers went to Canada to avoid it, but he didn't. So the Colonel was sent to Vietnam and he served there and in Laos and in Cambodia. What did he do? Don't know. The fighting was all over that part of South East Asia. Millions of Vietnamese, Cambodians and Laotians died and some 58, 000 American service men died. Life was cheap, I guess and the Colonel lost lots of his friends and I suspect he killed people too. It seems he never talks about the actual War itself ever.

In that part of the world heroin poppies are grown and, in fact, some US troops got hooked on it while they were there. Heroin is a good cash crop if you have very little. The rewards are bigger than growing other more sensible things. Of course the people farming it get very little money in comparison to the people selling it on. Like Francine and Fintan. On its journey to say Hammingbrum, each person who handles it takes their cut and it becomes more and more expensive. Also with each leg it gets less pure. The product gets corrupted. Oh look white powder - how can we make it go further? Oh, yes, baking powder looks the same - very cheap Very cheap in Tescos. Let's add that. Or look this rat poison is very cheap, let's add some of that then. Good idea.

Anyway, the Colonel, now a sergeant, thinks that he might be able to get a piece of the action. He knows that there is a market for heroin in the States. This market has increased with the returning soldiers who have had their first drug experiences in Vietnam, Cambodia, Laos and, of course, Thailand. So he needs a way of getting the heroin into the US. Planes are going back home all the time and very sadly many are returning with the bodies of soldiers killed in action. One of his mate's dies and they return his body to his home town of San Franscisco and the Colonel, he's not really a colonel, but let's call him that, he gets to escort the body home, because he's a friend. Anyway, he knows some vets in San Franciso that is it. He put s few little packets of heroin in pockets of the dead friend. It works well and bit by bit he expands. He starts to export heroin in coffins with the dead service men. He employs other service men both in Hanoi and in the States to pack and unpack the drugs. This is how his empire started. When he came to the UK and was stationed at Greenham he said he was a Colonel. He has probably never been a Colonel. He probably got the idea because he likes to eat a certain type of chicken that is finger licking good. Granfran fell for him or maybe his money. By that time he was employing Thai carpenters to make furniture and to hollow it out to make room for the heroin. After Aunty Bobby and Mum were born, the Colonel left for Mexico and then Colombia'

'Good God.' Chris whispers.

'That is really horrid. To put drugs into the coffins of the dead comrades. That takes some nerve. What a despicable man.'

149

'Yes and my father. My father that is who Ruby is talking about.'

'So thank God, you two seem to have somehow or other managed to survive, shall we say, difficult parenting, grandparenting... It must have been impossible being bullied by your mother, Leslie. How did you survive unscathed ?' I say.

With that Leslie stands up and takes off the cardigan part of her twin set. She rolls up the sleeves of the sweater to show severe cut marks on both arms - my prison visits tell me that these are scars from self mutilation. Also on the inner elbow, there are the unmistakeable jag marks of prolonged needle use. Leslie has injected into these arms over a long period of time. Seeing the damaged limbs makes me realise the extent of Leslie's drug habit.

'Heroin?' I ask.

'Yes, but I'm clean. Nearly five months. Nearly. Ruby has helped me. Haven't you Ruby? Now it's my turn to help Ruby. Help her with her baby. Yes, I will help her.'

I am speechless. 14 years? 14 years.

While I have been going on with my career and having a pretty good time in many ways, this filthy shit has been going on so close to me. My mother's sister's daughter has been the mastermind of a drugs ring. Her daughter has been an addict and I had no idea. Little innocent me. This poor bullied woman has taken refuge in heroin. She is on the road to recovery, but... Ruby has spent much of her life being a young carer to her poor bullied addict mother. Too late for regrets, it's more than time to help these women. I'll help in whatever way I can now.

It must be time for lunch. Steven and I go into the kitchen to prepare sardines on toast. There's enough for us all. I won't have to do my loaves and fishes trick.

I am surprised that there aren't knocks on the door, nor bricks through the window. I love my house and I've always felt safe here. But at the moment with all the comings and goings, I feel very exposed here. We are being left alone, I think, because Francine is in hospital. Fintan and Bobby are probably there with her now. With Francine seriously ill, the business has lost its momentum. Fintan won't be interested in hounding Ruby. he just does that because Francine tells him to. He just wants to go his own way. He doesn't care about Ruby's baby one way or another and he certainly doesn't want Ruby to take over the business that he has been running for Francine. In fact, it has served his purpose to have a terrified Ruby live int he woods.

And another interesting point - what role does Bobby have in all this shit? I've always thought of Bobby as bland. A beige person. We have bumped into each other quite regularly in Sainsburys. That's before I've got them to deliver. My hip means that it is difficult to go around the shops. Also they don't take too kindly to Steven, even though I pretend to be very deaf and tell them he is a hearing dog. They would be much more sympathetic if I was blind and he was a guide dog. Peeing on the cat food gondola didn't help. Once a mistake, but every week... The women there said that there was nothing very much to listen to in Sainsburys. I might miss out on some offers, but having Steven there for me would make no difference. Steven has no way of telling me that there is a special 3 for 2 on crumpets.

Yes, Bobby is just off white. She has very little conversation, though she can be quite brittle. Fat, but brittle with it, all in an overwhelming shade of ecru. She always seems to have a child hanging round her neck, but she is another one who drives an enormous Audi. I remember an inmate in prison asking me what I drive and I said a Nissan Micra and he said that his wife wouldn't be seen driving anything less than a BMW and that she changed it every year. Yes, changed it using the proceeds from his life of crime.

It was becoming obvious that we would only be safe when Francine, Fintan and Charlie were at her Majesty's pleasure. We need a plan. We need to ship them. We need to somehow get them in the do do without implicating us.

Chris came in and saw the sardine tins.

'i don't do fish, Nancy. It gives me the heebie jeebies. I know it's good for you and everything, but it makes me heave. I think we need a plan to put that lot inside. None of us are safe. That Francine might be in hospital now, but for how long? We need a plan.'

'Exactly, Chris. We need a plan. Baked beans Ok for you?'

I read the latest postcard over my fish. Postcard of the Taj Mahal, Agra from Suz Bedgegood. It looks like someone has nibbled a corner of it.

Hello Nancy Old Girl,

Didn't realise I was visiting a mausoleum. Hot, dusty and too many people. Too many people trying to sell me a Taj Mahal ashtray. I don't smoke. No pet dogs here.

Alvida, Suz xx

Mausoleum? It all comes down to death.

Chapter Eighteen

The four of us eat in silence to the sound of Steven's snores. The smell of sardines is not enough to wake him up. Too much excitement for him.

Chris has an idea.

'Why don't we go to Stratford?'

'You think a trip to the Royal Shakespeare Company might be a good idea when we are in a fix. I've never got on very well with Bill and it does seem inappropriate to...'

'No, I don't mean go to the theatre, though it might be nice. I mean if we go to the All Day Breakfast and take a trip towards Stratford on the Stratford Canal, it might give us a bit of breathing space and time to plan our next move.'

'Does Fintan know that we are friends? I don't think he does. Charlie goes up and down the Cesterrow and Hammingbrum Canal. He knows that we are friendly, but I don't know -what do you think girls? Shall we go on a trip to Stratford Upon Avon?'

'I think it's an idea. Why not? Mum? Yes? Ok let's do it, but I must be back by next week I have a hospital appointment next week. You know the baby, a scan and all that. I can't miss it.' Ruby says.

'No, of course. Oh a scan. How exciting! It's all so clever now, isn't it? Girl? Boy? Girl? Boy? Twins? Does it have all the right bits? It is all so very clever. Though i wouldn't want to know if it was a girl or boy - I'd like a nice surprise. I think.'

'Five minutes to get ready Ok. I'll ring for a taxi for you lot. I'll cycle over to the boatyard, so we have it if needs be. Bring tinned fish, Nancy. I have a good stock of most things, but I haven't any fish. I'm sure of that. You and Steven will have to eat it on deck, the smell will have me puking. I'll leave now and I'll probably be there before you. OK?'

As Leslie, Ruby, Steven and I are walking up to the road to pick up the taxi. My mobile rings. It's Beryl my cousin and Francine's sister. She is crying.

'Nancy, oh Nancy, it's Francine. It's her heart it's very weak. Very weak. She's had a heart attack. She's in intensive care and they don't (sob) think she is going to last...last until...last until... I am trying to find Leslie and Ruby. The need to be here. Here at the hospital - the QE. They need to be here, before it's too late. She's going, Nancy. She is going and I know that you never got on, but... she's leaving us, Nancy. She isgoing to go and she needs to have her daughters by her side. Bobby is in Florida with the children for a bit of sun, so it has to be Leslie. Leslie and Ruby. They need to be here now. Before it's too late. I am here, of course, but she needs her nearest and dearest.She loves Leslie and Ruby so much.'

'Ok, Beryl, I'll do my best. I'll see if I can find them for you. OK?' I hang up.

'Right, Leslie, Ruby. That's Beryl. She's at the QE. Francine is in intensive care and it looks as though she won't survive much longer. It's going to be curtains soon. Bobby and the kids are somewhere in the Keys swanning it and Beryl feels you should be there. Do you want to go and see someone who has dominated your lives and made them a misery die?' I ask.'Beryl actively wants you there. Don't punish Beryl.'

And Ruby says ' OK. Yes, I want to make sure she has gone.'

'If she goes so do... so do... so do I. What about... what about the boat? Chris and the black pudding?'

'It's the All Day Breakfast, Leslie. I'll send Chris a text saying we will be a bit longer than we thought. Shall I tell him where we are? I'm too slow with this texting thing - I shan't bother. I suppose we could be sometime. I'd like to know where Fintan is actually. He's not in   Florida with Bobby and the kids. Fancy taking four children out of school in term time, I ask you?'

We four get in the taxi that is, for once, quite prompt and head off to the QE Hospital. I realise that I won't be able to take Steven into intensive care as a hearing dog. This won't work. Khaver Khan the taxi driver knows me and I put quite a bit of custom his way, so I ask him to take Steven to the boatyard and to take him to the All Day Breakfast and Chris.

My mobile goes and it's Beryl again.

'Have you found them, Nancy? It would be so awful for a dear God fearing woman to die without her immediate family with her. She needs to know that they care. After all the problems they have given her. Do you know where they are for God sake!'

'They are with me, Beryl.'

'Put that Jezebel on the phone, Nancy. Do it now. I mean it. I want to give her a piece of my...'

'Oh, the signal's going Beryl' and I hang up.

Khaver gets us to the hospital and we all give a puzzled Steven big kisses and Khaver drives off with him. It takes us ages to find intensive care. Do you remember when hospitals had lines on the floor that you could follow them to get to the place you are looking for? This is a neat idea.

It works well. So why is it that all the brand spanking new hospitals I have been in have decided that it is not a good way of finding your way around. Eventually a nice woman with a trolley gives us instructions we understand and we make it to ICU. Beryl is in the waiting area. She tells the nurse that Leslie and Ruby are Francine's daughter and granddaughter and off they go into the ward. Only two at a time, so I miss out on the dying scene. It seems that Francine is unconscious. It seems that Ruby could not help herself. She gave me a run through afterwards. It seems she whispered with a smile on her face in Granfran's ear something like the following.

'You have bullied my dear Mum all her life. You haven't one ounce of humanity. You allow her to take chemicals that Fintan said would make her feel better. They didn't and it has taken me and lots of help from Aquarius to get her off the filthy stuff. You have made my life a misery. I am horrified that you want me to kill my baby and that you want me to run the business that has destroyed so many lives.'

Leslie and Ruby came out of the ward and into the waiting area with their arms around each other, crying. I was surprised, but I think it was relief, rather than grief. Beryl burst into tears when she saw them, because she knew it was the end for the sister that she loved.There is no doubt in my mind that naive Beryl loved Francine. Though I can't be sure that Francine loved Beryl.

Fintan rushes in. Leslie and Ruby sink, wide eyed, but look for a way out.

'Has she gone? She can't go yet. Bobby's not here. She's on a plane, but it's a bloody long flight. She can't have gone yet.'

He rounds on me.

'She was at yours, you bitch! He told me the ambulance driver. They couldn't find it. You did something to her. What did you do to Francine. Tell me! Tell me now!'

He has invaded my personal space. He spits out the words and slavers into my mouth right close. Oh, to have a dental drill.

A woman in a green paper suit bounds in and is just about to restrain Fintan when she sees me.

'Professor, it is so good to see you after all this time. Remember me, I was at the Dental Hospital part time when my kids were little. It is so good to see you. Oh dear, are you a relative of poor Mrs Byrde. It was very quick and pain free at the end.'

This takes the wind out of Fintan's sails, but not for long. He is just about to jab his pointy finger in my shoulder when Leslie floors him and shouts -'quick!'

Leslie, Ruby and me run through a door and end up in a cupboard full of cardboard bowls and bedpans. There is no way out. The drop from the window is several storeys. Ruby is quick. Armed with a full pan, she throws open the door. Fintan is sitting down, holding his head.

'Take a step back all of you. This is full of poo and I will throw it over you if you come closer.'

Fintan stands up and Ruby throws the contents of the pan at him. Beryl and nice nurse seem frozen to the ground.

'Stay there, Uncle Fintan, Aunty Beryl, kind person. We are leaving'.

And with that, we do.

We don't leave the hospital right away. Ruby needs a pee and wants to give her hands a thorough wash, so we find a disabled toilet and all go in. We all have a pee and wash our hands and use that gel stuff from a squirter on the wall. I look out to see if it's all clear. I am feeling a bit knackered with my hip, so we pick up a wheelchair and Leslie pushes me with Ruby on my lap. We eventually find the way out and the taxi rank.

We go by taxi to the boatyard and find Chris and Steven chatting to Khaver Khan over a dram of whiskey. He's never been on a narrowboat before, so Chris has been giving him a guided tour and showing him the ropes. They are mulling over the possibility of Khaver buying his son, who is at university, a boat to live on. It would be cheaper than a house, but he would still have it as an investment when Ahmed finishes his PHD.

When the space is invaded by us, hysterical women, Khaver takes his leave and Chris promises to have a look out for a nice little craft that might suit the student life style for Khaver.

'Francine has died, Chris.' I say, 'Leslie and Ruby were with her.'

'Good really. We know she is well and truly gone.' Ruby rubs her eyes.

'It is such a relief. Yes, it is a relief. Yes, on one hand, but when someone, you know like your mother, someone you've know all your life dies, dies forever, I feel a terrible, yes, terrible hole, a   terrible sense of, well, loss. Not so much a loss of the person, she wasn't a very nice mother to me, you know, but a loss of what, sort of, might have been. She could have been a nice mum, couldn't she? She could have been. Now she'll never be a good mother. I needed a good mum, I think. It would have been nice to have had a nice mum.' Leslie sobs inconsolably .

It's time for tea with a snorter of scotch and Chris makes some sarnies to fill a gap.The ham is Ok, but it's not tuna.

We know that Francine is dead. We know that Fintan is very much alive and thinks that we are responsible in some way for her death. Not sure if he thinks we have bumped her off, or what? The good news is that there is no pressure on Ruby to take over the drug business reins from Granfran. Ruby won't have any pressure from Fintan. Fintan will want it all for himself and I presume Bobby. Bobby - what a silly name for a grown woman?

And Bobby is on her way home to the UK from the Keys with her children who should be in school.

'Where does Bobby go to on holiday, Leslie? Does she always go to the same place?' I ask.

'Yes, they stay, I'm told, Mother says, it's very lovely, yes, they stay in the beach house in the Keys in Florida. It's right on the beach, you know, the sand is just there. Next to the house.'

'Fintan said that she's flying back·now. ' Puts in Ruby.

'Right, so we have Bobby returning. Fintan in a tizz. Charlie we don't know where exactly
is but the Lazy Daze is being mended here at the boatyard. In fact, he could be very close to us now, couldn't he?'

'Yes, he could indeed. Shall I see if I can track him down,' offers Chris.

'Yes, good idea. What do we want to happen? What do we want to do now? What, as they say, outcomes do we want and need to, go forward?'

Ruby suggest we make a list and we do.

The List

1. *Ruby's baby must be a priority - so keeping Ruby safe is imperative.*
2. *All of us to be free from any involvement in the drugs trade.*
3. *All of us to be free from Fintan and his cronies, this includes Charlie - this means shipping them to the police with enough evidence for him to go down for a very long time.*

4. *Evidence of Fintan's misdemeanors should not reflect on us at all.*
5. *Any possible inheritance from Francine should go, not to Ruby and Leslie, but into drug rehab for addicts.*
6. *Leslie and Ruby should stay with me and Steven until the baby is born.*
7. *We should be kind to Beryl and Bobby (this was put in by Leslie). Also find out how much they know about the drugs thing (this was put in by me, because I am just interested).*
8. *We should try and keep Geoff the angler out of any shit, because he had been very kind to both Leslie and Ruby, in his way.*
9. *We should be kind to Chris (this was put in by me).*
10. *We should all live happily ever after (again put in by Leslie).*

We decide that this was a good list to start with and for some reason that I'm not sure about, we decide to meet Bobby's plane at the airport to tell her about the death of Francine. Chris looks up the internet on his phone. Phone? I ask you. I liked it when you could just ring someone up. Anyway, there is a flight arriving from Tampa airport in about two hours. We decide rightly or wrongly that we are going to meet it. This might mean that we are sorting out number 7 on the list. Maybe.

'It's a shame you haven't got a car, Nance' says Ruby.

'Oh I have got a car. I just can't drive it, because of my hip. It gives me gip.'

'You do? I could drive it. I drove the Audi before. The night of the escape from Granfran's that was fun' says Ruby.

'My car is a Micra. It hasn't been driven for sometime, but it will probably start. Perhaps? But you are definitely not driving it, Ruby. You are underage with no bits of paper and you are pregnant - you probably won't fit behind the wheel.'

'That is unkind.'

'Chris can drive it. I think he can drive,' I know he can drive. He drove the Audi into the canal.

Khaver Khan is called to take us to the garage around the corner from the house where my trusty Micra is parked. I have the keys on my house keys, so all is well. Khaver seems a bit upset that I won't need his services anymore, but...

Chris gets behind the wheel and the engine springs into life. We are all very pleased, because the car is covered with a thick layer of dust. Leslie takes off her cardy and uses it as a duster. I say thank you and that it will wash Ok on a woollen wash.

We wave goodbye to Khaver who reminds Chris about the finding him a boat for his son, as we pile into the car. I get the front passenger seat, because it is my car.

'Hammingbrum International Airport - step on the gas!'

The traffic is busy, but it's 25 minutes, not so bad.

We get there with time to spare, the flight is due in twenty minutes. After it arrives of course you have all that other stuff, when you arrive at an airport you have to go through customs and then wait for your baggage - it all takes ages.

We are going to be charged an enormous amount in the car park.

We go for a coffee and milkshake.

' I don't know whether to drink this or go for a swim in it.' I say.

I keep an eye open for either Fintan, Beryl or even Charlie, maybe? I have a feeling that someone will come to meet Bobby and the children to both meet her and to break the news about her mother's death. You don't want someone to tell you that in a text or on the phone call. Then I spot her. Beryl in black from head to toe. Well, I suspect that Bobby will guess from that.

'Don't look now, but there's Beryl.'

'Where?'

'Over by Smith's. She looks like an extra from a funeral in the Godfather.'

'Do we go and chat - pass the time of day?' asks Chris. 'Or just ignore her?'

I really don't know. I might have guessed she'd be there. Of course, she would there to meet her sister.

'You stay here and finish your drinks. I'll join that queue over there and get her attention and have a chat to her.'

'Why?'

I ignore that, because I have no idea why. Or maybe I do. I think I should gauge Beryl's response to the hospital fiasco.

I join a queue and wave in Beryl's direction.

'Going away somewhere nice?'

'Yes.'

'I hear it is very nice in Dusseldorf.'

I look up at the board at the head of the queue and see that I am going to Dusseldorf. Is that Germany? I think it is.

Chapter Nineteen

'So are you here to meet Bobby and the children? They're back very soon, aren't they?'

'Yes, terrible news of course. She will be devastated. She and Francine were very close, you know. Closer than Francine and Leslie. Well, let's be honest there was always an, shall we say, an intellectual gap between Francine and Leslie.'

'Really?'

'Strange do at the hospital. Totally inappropriate. I know that Leslie can't help herself, being you know, a little, shall we say, weak in the head. She's come up with some strange stories from time to time, but Francine has been very good and sent her on retreats and things to help her mental well-being. I suppose I should think - poor girl, but it is difficult to hold your tongue and it lets the family down.'

How hard is it to keep your mouth shut? I am very good. I am tempted, but I keep schum.

'Well, give Bobby my love won't you. And of course, my condolences, Beryl.'

'Yes, of course dear. And enjoy Dusseldorf. Hope you'll be back in time for the funeral. It will be fun.'

I wait until she'd gone to Arrivals. Then I return to the coffee shack, I find the others sitting on the floor hiding.

'So Beryl is meeting Bobby. We don't need to be here. And now I've suggested that I am flying to Dusseldorf.'

'Dusseldorf - wow!' Says Ruby.

'I've always wanted to go to Dusseldorf.' Says Chris.

'Oh yes and I believe you. Thousands wouldn't.'

''No really - I like water. I like canals. I like rivers. Dusseldorf is on the river Dussel, you know, Dussel, Dusseldorf. It's close to the Erft and on the Lower Rhine Basin. I would love to go to Dusseldorf.'

'Well, you are not going now matey.'

'Having come all this way, I think I want to see the reunion between Beryl and Bobby. See how much Bobby cries.' Says Ruby.

'Oh yes, she will cry and cry. I just know it.' Adds Leslie.

'What to do? I know. If we go to the other Starfucks that is just by the Arrival. We can have another drink and watch what happens. We can watch Bobby's reaction to Beryl's widow's weeds and all her news. We can see if the children's manners have improved which I doubt. Beryl thinks I'm going to Dusseldorf, so with me not around, Fintan may think that one small thorn in his side has gone on hols for a bit. Look, the monitor says that the luggage from the Tampa flight is in the baggage hall. Let's get another coffee.' I say.

'I could do with one of those Almond Croissants.' Ruby says hopefully.

Lots of people are waiting for the flight to come through, so we are like chameleons. There are four flights coming through, business people from Brussels, large Indian families on the Dubai link from Delhi, a package tour from Ibiza with young people looking sunburnt and ill and the wealthy in white slacks and Armani sunglasses returning from a little sun in Key West. No Bobby and family. There is no Bobby and no kids. They are not coming through. The Tampa flight goes off the top of the screen. It no longer exists. There is no Bobby, Brenda, Basil, Bertie and Barbara. Don't you just hate it when people give their children names starting with the same letter? I do. I just hate it so much, it hurts.

We all duck down when we see that Beryl has turned away and leaves, shoulders' hunched. Beryl has left the building. We wait. We eat Almond Croissants.

Then behind a mountain of suitcases on a trolley topped by toddler twins, we see a woman with tango skin, being followed by two sullen, slow children. The woman, Bobby, stops and turns.

'Get a bloody move on!'

I rush up and greet them all with a smile.

'Bobby my dear, Leslie and Ruby are here to greet you. Maybe, we could sit over here for a moment. Sadly we have some difficult news.'

'It's that bastard Fintan, isn't it? What's happened? Where's Mother? She always picks me up at the airport when he can't get his arse here. I've told Mother that I cannot cope much longer. I get a message to get back home asap and look, he's not here. Just whimpy Les and Ruby no knickers. And you Nance - after your strip show at my wedding - you fucking cow - I'm bloody surprised that you have the nerve to come anywhere near me, because if I had the strength I would deck you here and now. Bren, Baz take a twin each and take them to the toilet, they are jigging about a bit and they need to wee. And I mean now! Like now! I mean it! Mother isn't answering her bloody phone. I know she pretends not to know how to use the damn thing, but I know she can. Where the hell is she?'

I can't resist it.

'She's dead, Bobby.'

She ignores the information.

'Leslie, where is Mother? She said she'd be here like normal. Fintan never makes the bloody airport. He hates anything to do with flying and airports are full of bloody aeroplanes, aren't they? He gets nauseous just climbing a step ladder - the wanker. I tell you that when I get my hands on Mother, I will give her a piece of my mind. Flying with these four little shits across the Atlantic is absolute bloody hell. Leslie, where is Mother? I want to be home now!'

'Sit down, Bobby. Sit down on this case. This big one. Sit down, Bobby. Did you hear, did you hear what Nancy said. She said that Mother is dead. She's dead Bobby. Me and Ruby were with her at the hospital. She had a heart attack. Her heart went dicky. And she died in the QE. The new one. Me and Ruby were there, Bobby. We were.' Leslie tells her.

The truth hit Bobby like a sledge hammer.

'Where's Fintan?   I want to see her. I want to see her. I want to see Mother. I want to see my Mother. I want Fintan.'

'Fintan was at the hospital. Put your mobile on. You can now, Bobby. You can ring him.'

Fintan will have his mobile on in the hospital or anywhere. Do you have to turn a mobile off in a hospital now? You used to have to do it. In intensive care you probably have to because of all those electronic gismos, but Francine won't be in intensive care anymore. She will have been moved to somewhere very cold like a fridge.

I'm getting a bit worried about Steven. We left him in the car. I told him he was guarding it from terrorists and he was happy with that. Happy in the short term. They are funny about dogs in airports. They point you to quarantine kennels. Being a hearing dog doesn't work and he can't cut the mustard as a drug sniffer dog because of his size and gammy leg - for that he needs to grow into a German Shepherd.

'Fintan, where are you?' Bobby barks into her phone. 'At home? Why aren't you here....Here at the airport. ...Here meeting me.... I'm back.... We're back....Where's Mother? ...Yes, I know, Leslie's here....Yes, she had the decency to tell me.... She did what to you?.... She wouldn't do that - I know my sister... Come on Fintan, you're having a laugh....No Beryl isn't here....I'm very sorry, but no, she isn't here....Leslie's here with her girl and that shit who ruined our wedding and there's this bloke here too....I've no idea who he is or why he's here.'

'Chris, this is Bobby. Bobby this is Chris.'

'Pleased to meet you, Chris.' Bobby interrupts her call and then returns to it. 'So - how are we supposed to get

170

home... taxi with all this stuff....And where is Mother?... Chapel of Rest in Balsall Heath?....What do you mean the one in Bastedge was full?...Full my arse.... So, I get a taxi home...I can't pay, I've only got dollars....You better be at home when I get back or.....'

Bobby throws her phone. Ruby picks it up and gives it back to her. Leslie puts her arms around her for consolation.

Baz, I believe that is what he is called, comes back with two twins.

'Where's Bren? ' Bobby asks.

'Dunno.' Baz answers.

'You've lost her, you stupid little shit.'

'I got both twins.' Baz smiles.

'I am not having a good time, Basil. Go find your sister this minute. We've got to get home quick. Granfran is dead....'

Basil's face crumples and he starts to cry. Cry, sob, howl.

'Shut up now. She was my mother, not yours.'

I turn to Chris and whisper -'This side of the family are less sensitive than mine.'

We are now causing a bit of a stir among a group of Japanese students who have just arrived from the baggage hall. I have to take control.

'I'm concerned for you Bobby. Chris will help you to the taxi rank and put you and these three children in a taxi home. We will look for the other one...Bren? We will have just enough space for her in with us and we will drop her off on our way....'

'I'll help with the kids' says Ruby

Chris is a gem. He pushes the trolley and Bobby and Ruby takes the kids. Leslie and I look at each other. Where is Brenda? We check the toilets. We check the cafes and shops. Then, over the tannoy

'Good evening ladies and gentlemen, this is your captain, Captain Brenda Flannery speaking. I want to welcome you aboard this Bicycle Airways flight 123 service from Hammingbrum International Airport to Spaghetti Junction. Your Co-pilot today is ...is? Sorry we don't have one - it's all down to me. And our Chief Flight Attendant is...oh it's me again - I'll be around with the sarnies in a bit. Once we get airborne today, our flight time will be 5 hours and 27 minutes; currently there is very heavy air traffic,so our flight speed will be about 3 miles per hour and we will be flying at about 50 centimetres. The winds are out of the South at 12 MPH, poor visibility, thunder clouds, torrential rain and the temperature is -2 degrees centigrade. This is not Florida, I repeat this is not Florida. We'll get back to you en route just as soon as we have more information; once again, welcome aboard.'

It's Brenda.

Where is the tannoy? Where is it? I ask at a shop and get a blank look. The assistant hasn't got English as a second language. I ask at the Hertz Car Hire and they point in the direction of a door. It has one of those number buttons security thingies. Luckily, staff are rushing through and we join them. And there is Brenda behind a microphone. A man goes to manhandle her. She takes a bite out of his hand.

'Put her down.' I say.

'Very sorry for this, sir, madam, she's my niece, Bren....my niece Brenda. I need to take her home now. Very sorry for any....'

And Brenda says' I've never seen these women before in my life.'

She sits back in the seat and everyone looks at me and Leslie.

'I am being groomed for the white slave trade.' says the little liar.

This actually misfires. All the airport staff that are in that room would like Brenda to be taken off to somewhere remote and horrid.

The man that Bren bit says 'take her, good luck and welcome to her.'

She reluctantly walks out with us to where we last saw Chris and Ruby and there they are. So we go back to the car. Then I realise that I have the parking ticket. Chris and I go to the machine, leaving Ruby, Leslie and Bren to remove the turd on the back seat and to then shoehorn the three of them and Steven into the back.

We put the card into the machine and it says £15. This is ridiculous. We are horrified. Between us, we find £15 in change and put in the machine. It comes back and tells us that the ticket is in the wrong way. Turn ticket over it tells us. We do so and it tells us to turn the ticket over. I press the button to talk to someone. Amazingly someone answers straight away.

'Yes.' The voice says.

'We've put money in and it tells us to put the ticket up the other way.

'Use the other machine.' The voice goes away.

We are not going to use the other machine, because we have already put £15 into this machine.

We take the ticket and presume we can get out of the car park, because we have paid.

The car is rammed in the back, so Chris and I are lucky to have the front. I think that Steven will come and jump on my lap, but he likes to be squashed with the women. He is a bit of a tart.

We get to the barrier of the car park and Chris puts the ticket in the machine. And the message comes up - *£53 owing. Pay at the machine.*

This is outrageous and we have had a bit of a day and want to go home or anywhere. Chris presses the button to talk to someone. There is no voice. No one answers.

I am very tired and it is the last straw. I get out and address the CCTV Camera.

'We are very tired and we put £15 into the ticket machine. The ticket machine told us to put the ticket in the other way. We did this and it asked us to turn it again. We had a brief conversation with a voice and he told us to use the other machine, but we had already paid on that machine. We want to leave this carpark and the message her says that we should pay £53 - we do not owe £53 This is not right and there is no one here that will talk to us, so I am raising the bar. Do you hear me? I am raising the bar. I am raising this barrier so that we can exit.'

I turn to Chris and tell him to drive under the barrier.

'It's too low Nancy. The car won't go under that.'

So I pull the barrier up further and it breaks off in my hands. I get in the car and Chris accelerates and we drive off. Those in the back seat are stunned. Chris giggles while I fume.

We head to the All Day Breakfast. We all like the idea of being invisible. And we all feel that it's easier to be invisible on the boat rather than at my house.

Chapter Twenty

I wake up in the morning by the smell of kippers, but it isn't kippers, it is in fact bacon sarnies. This is my second best breakfast and for the others, except for Steven, it is probably number one.

'I'll take you home, Brenda, when we've finished eating. OK? I should have taken you home last night, but I forgot. Did anyone text Bobby?'

'No.'

'I have to take you home, Bren. I do. You should be with your parents.'

'No.'

'Why not, Brenda? Everyone has rows with their mum and dad when they are growing up. I know I did.' Says Chris.

'What's the specific problem, Bren.' Says Ruby.

'I'm at risk.' Says Brenda.

No one wants to ask any further questions, because Brenda looks very solemn.

We pour more tea and open a packet of Hobnobs for seconds.

'Ok, Francine has died.' I start to recap information.

'What?' Says Bren.

'She died yesterday.' Ruby says 'Mum and I were with her. Of course you were playing silly buggers when we told Bobby.'

'How did she died?'

'Heart attack - natural causes.'

'No way. Granfran died of natural causes. I don't believe it. Well, that is a relief. Bet Dad's a bit pleased. He can take over the dynasty now, can't he?' Says Brenda.

'You know about the business?' I ask.

'Of course, I live in that house. In theory, we live in our house, you know, but really we live with Granfran. We are always there, aren't we? We all live in different bits of it when we stay over, which is almost alway. different bits, but we all are in the same building. We never really see much of each other, but we are all there. Aunty Leslie and Rubes in the attic. Us lot on the two top stairs and then Granfran on the ground floor and the business in the basement.'

'So, what goes on, then Brenda. What is the business? What is it? Is it, well I don't know. Do you know what it's all about, Bren. Do you know? Do you?' Leslie waffles on.

'It's import and export.' Confirms Brenda.

'Import and export what?' Chris ventures.

'Drugs, of course. I am an expert, though my body is a temple.'

'How old are you, Brenda?' Chris is puzzled.

'I will be 12 next birthday. I am still in junior school. There is nothing they can teach me anymore. I am just biding my time.' Bren says.

'I know all about the business. If fact, I used to do some mixing for Granfran for riding lessons.'

'What?' I am finding all of this very disturbing.

'Yes, as you might know, dealers mix drugs with other stuff to make more of a profit.' Says Bren.

'Really?' Says Chris.

'Oh yes, and I used to mix baking powder with amphetamine. Yeh, Saturday morning down in the basement. A bit of mixing and then using the pill making thing. And if Granfran was happy, it would be off to riding in the afternoon. It's good to mix it a bit. Illegal drugs should, of course, not be too pure. If stuff is too pure then people often die.'

'That is very true. Very true. Do you remember...what's his name? I went to school with him and his brother. His brother was called. I can't remember. They lived... They lived around the corner from school. Their mum was a dinner lady. Yes, she was. She was nice because she would always give you seconds if you ask, sort of asked nicely. Yeh, she was lovely.' Leslie is wittering on.

'Don't worry Mum.' Says Ruby.

'Some very young people do take drugs. Some very young ones like you, Brenda. Have you? I mean it must be difficult.' I ask.

Poor kid, how do we carry on with this? Well, we have to, of course. This is so important. It is obvious that we have to make a move soon. Brenda needs to be sheltered from all this shit. And of course, so do her brothers and sister.

'What do you want, Brenda? What do you want to happen now? Your grandmother has died. There will be a funeral soon I suppose. You know that your dad is heavily involved with it all and maybe your mum? Is your Mum involved? Or even Beryl too?' I ask.

'Being involved and knowing are different to wanting to take part'. Ruby says. 'Mum and I don't want anything to with this business. Mum didn't want to take heroin and or anything else, but it is very difficult to avoid it when it consumes most of your family. You know all of this, because it's your reality. It is how life is. It just is. Some children have a nice mum and dad and they live in a nice house and everything is normal. For some people things are so un-normal that it stinks. When you have grown up in a world of corruption, then that is what life is. You adapt and you try and make sense of what is happening. It is a terrible strain. I don't think I can carry on like this. I told a teacher at school once and she said that I had a very creative imagination. She said I should write for the telly.'

'We have two pressing problems. One is to keep Brenda safe from the so many things that are going on - when I say Brenda that includes her siblings too.' I say. 'And we need to expose what is happening in Bastedge. It may be that we could do a big reveal at the next big social event. You know at Francine's funeral.'

'When is it?'

'We don't know yet, Mum, do we?'

Wise old Chris says 'it's summer. It will be fairly soon, because you don't have the same wait as you do in winter. In winter, more people die, so there is a longer queue for burial or cremation. In winter, bodies stack up. Also bodies rot quicker in the warmth.'

'Ring Aunty Beryl, Mum and ask her about the funeral. - yeh?' Says Ruby.

'I don't like to.'

'This is your Mother we are talking about and she's asking you to ring your Aunty. This is easy, Leslie.'

'You do it then.' Brenda says to Ruby.

'Ok Bren, I will ring Aunty Beryl. ' Says Ruby.

'Yer a coward, Ruby. Yes, you ring Aunty Beryl - give her my love. No, don't do that. If you do that then she'll know I'm with you. At the moment they'll think I'm still at the airport.' Says Brenda.

Ruby presses the number.

'Hello Aunty Beryl?....yes, it's me Ruby.... Did Brenda turn up?....No?..... Who's saying she's flown to Venezuela?.... She was spotted on a plane to Heathrow...and they think she's on a plane to....Ok....It seems very unlikely to me....I don't think she likes flying....Anyway, I'm very upset about Granfran...I suppose it was fairly sudden.... When is the funeral likely to be?...Right....Ok....Thank you....Let me know about Brenda....Yes, she is a very independent and imaginative girl....Yes, I like her a lot....Say hi to everyone....Mum and I will be there of course. No, I know we sometimes didn't see eye to eye, yes, but.....Ok speak to you soon...'

'Venezuala? I'm in Venezuela.'

'Yeh, a girl matching your description was seen getting on a flight to Heathrow and then onto a flight to the Simon Bolivar Airport in Caracas. It seems that Caracas is in Venezuela.' Says Ruby.

'That's real cool.' Brenda is very pleased.

'This is very dodgy. Chris and I could be done for abduction. You have to go back home now and don't bring us into it. I'm not sure what you can say, but...'

'I am very creative, Nancy. I write good stories.'

'When is the funeral?' I ask.

'They had a cancelation, so it's this Friday.'

'A cancelation?' Chris is puzzled.

'We need to expose this drug ring. We are all agreed on this. Oh you are agreed aren't you, Brenda?' I say.

'Oh yes, Nance - it has to stop.'

'So let's plan everything for this Friday - everything around the day of Francine's funeral. Give her a bloody good send off.' I say.

'If you believe, if you believe in God, that's a Christian God, not another one. You know like Allah and such. If you believe in Jesus and that lot then she is in hell. She is already in hell. You know burning, burning forever and ever, Amen.' We all shudder at Leslie's words.

'Brenda - do you want to be our informer or a spy?' I ask.

'Oh yes, please Nance that would be so good. Yeh, I think a spy. I fancy that.'

'OK, we''ll get you a mobile phone so that you can send messages to us. We'll drop you at the Botanical Gardens and you can walk around the corner. You tell your Mum and Dad that you have walked from the airport, but slept on a bus shelter overnight - does that works as a story? Does it?' I say.

"They'll believe me. The best way of lying is to give loads of details. It works every time.' Brenda lies a lot it seems.

Chris has an old pay as you go phone. Brenda doesn't like it much because It hasn't got all the bells and whistles that a new one does, but never mind. Chris puts some credit on it and we take her to the Botanical Gardens - it's very cloak and dagger. If I had an Aston Martin with all the gadgets I would have given it to her.

Less than half an hour, Brenda rings up. She's crying. Her lying has been believed, but Bobby is more concerned about her not being at home to look after the twins. It seems the twins have missed her. They have spent time in their cots that they are too big for. So Brenda has walked straight into childcare issues. Poor kid. Another young carer.

Brenda rings again a couple of hours later.

'They've got Granfran in an open coffin in the hallway. I had to go and kiss her on the cheek.'

'Sounds like something out of the Godfather.' I say.

'Who's that?' Says Brenda. 'I don't know no Godfather. Anyway, the funeral starts from here at half past ten and we walk, yeh, walk around the corner to St George's, you know the Church place by the traffic lights. They are going to burn her. It's Lodge Hill Cremathingy, where ever that is? We kids are not invited to that - thank God, I don't want to see her go up in smoke, thank you very much. Mum wanted her to be buried, but it's too expensive, Dad says. So that's it - oh yes, then there's going to be food at the posh hotel at Fiveways. Anything else you want to know? Shit someone is coming...' The phone goes dead.

I leave it half and hour and ring back. No one answers. I leave a message to ring Josie from the school netball team - this is our code.

'We need to go to the police. And we need to go now.' I say to the others.

Leslie, Ruby, Chris, me and Steven walk up the road. There is a police station up by the roundabout. It is appears to be closed. We need to do whatever it is we are going to do immediately, because we have just got the boost to our courage, fearing for Brenda.

We get in the Micra and Chris drives us to Digbeth. It is open thank God. We go in. There is a queue of people. It is a very poor advert for modern policing - the place is scruffy and smells of a badly kept nursing home.

Then it's our turn.

'We want to talk to someone about drugs, please.' I say.

'Ah yes, Madam, unfortunately we don't sell them here. (Ha, ha, ha.) if you and your....erm....party would like to sit there, then I'd get someone from the Police Drug Intervention Programme to come and see you.'

This doesn't seem quite right to me.

We wait and wait some more and then a nice well-scrubbed young woman comes and introduces herself.

'I'm PC Deirdre McCall and I'm part of the Drugs Intervention Programme, we work with many different agencies to support addicts make significant changes to their lives. I don't think I've met any of you before.' She is looking us up and down. She would know that Leslie has a problem in the past if she took her teeth out.

'I'm not sure you are in the right department.'

'I assure you I am. What can I help you with?'

'We want to report the criminal importing and sale of illegal drugs over a 35 year period.' I say.

'Stay there. I'll get a detective.'

When he looks at us, he sees a travelling show. He sees an elderly and quaint couple of old dears, a very young pregnant girl and a youngish, but faded woman in a twinset and pearls plus a disabled dog. He listens politely.

'There is a house in the posh end of Bastedge that is the British business headquarters of an international drugs business. Three of us are related to the people who run it. The three of us are Leslie, who's mother is the big boss of the UK branch and Ruby her granddaughter. She is dead, the boss is dead, Francine Byrde is dead - funeral on Friday. Oh, natural causes. I'm her cousin. We are not close, not at all. No never been close. Oh yes, and Fintan is manager of lots of it and his daughter Brenda is back at home. Back of home - yes, there's a story around that too. Anyway, Brenda is 12 years old and passes us messages about what is going on. She's our spy.' I do the talking as usual.

He thinks we are talking out of our bottoms. Is there any thing that I can offer that might get him to take us seriously?

'See it must have started before Leslie was born. Her mother the infamous Francine met the Colonel...'

'The Colonel?'

'Yes, the Colonel.'

'The Colonel as in America? As in the Vietnam War? As in Coffins? As in the Cadaver Connection?'

'Absoluetly.'

'But that is all a story?'

'No, this is the Colonel's daughter here in Digbeth, here and now. Leslie Byrde is the Colonel's daughter - really she is."

'Go on?'

'Yes, I am. I am the daughter of Francine Byrde and the Colonel. It's true. Really really true. I can tell you all about it. I know all about it. We are not lying. I don't lie. we don't lie. We always tell the truth. Well, we usually tell the truth. Maybe a white lie sometimes, but we are here to tell you things and it has to stop. It all has to stop. We are so desperate. It has to stop. It has to stop now. Please, please believe us.' Says Leslie.

And with that, Leslie took the brave move that made the detective believe every word. She took off her cardigan and rolled up her sleeves to reveal the self mutilation marks and the inner elbow jag marks of her heroin abuse.

'I was at the comp and I was a good girl, I was, and I did what I was told. School was not nice and I didn't go too often. But home was horrible too.I felt very sad all the time. You know down, depressed. This boy tried it on. He tried it on and on and on and I felt poorly a bit and then I had this baby. She's lovely now. She saved me, but... Mother was ashamed of me. Mother is Francine Byrde like what Nancy said. She said I was scum. Our house was full of packages and Fintan told me that they had stuff in them that would make me feel better. And he started to give me stuff. All sorts of stuff, bit by bit. I think he use to experiment on me. You know. What does this tablet do. Let's put this in a smoke. Yeh.   Smoke this then Les, he'd say. See what is does to the poor stupid cow Leslie. That kind of thing. It lead to this'

Leslie mimed injecting into her arm.

 'They call it H, smack, skag, brown, junk, horse, gear, heroin.' With this Leslie crumples into Ruby's arms and Ruby finishes the story.

'Mum was 16 when I arrived in the school toilet. Before I was born, Mum was given odd bits of pills and cannabis by Uncle Fintan, but nothing hard. But when I was born, she wasn't allowed back in school, so she was at home all day with me. Granfran, that's my grandmother, Francine, was a total bitch. She bullied Mum and ridiculed her. How do I know that? I know because she has done that all my life. My mum was told she was scum, because of me, the bastard. She wasn't looked after properly by Granfran and she got pregnant without anyone telling her about sex. She grew up having to say yes to everything, so it was impossible for her to say no to men. After I was born, Uncle Fintan decided that that Mum was really good material for experimentation and that's when the real hard stuff came in. Aunty Beryl was kind to me, that's Francine's sister. I call her Aunty, but she's my Great Aunt really. Granfran sent me to a posh school. The idea was to make a lady of me. She wanted me to do well specifically in languages and later business studies, because she wanted me to be involved in the business. Why would I want any part of it when I could see what it doing to my Mum? Mum lived a life of abuse. I used to be invited to school friend's homes. but I never went, because I couldn't have anyone back to where I lived. Mum wasn't up for it and Granfran would have loved it, but I could not bear having her pretending to be nice. I tried it once.Just once. Once was enough. She bought everyone a My Little Pony and they thought she was great, but she wasn't, she was horrid. I looked after Mum as well as I could. But it was very hard. She would be great all sparkly and then desperate with puking and shakes. She is lucky to be alive. Thank goodness for Aquarius. I found out about them at school - you know a leaflet in the Health Awareness section in the library. Thank goodness for Aquarius, I say.'

'Hang on, let me get my colleagues.'

Chapter Twenty One

They interview us separately first of all, in little interview rooms. They tape the interviews. They have to wait ages to interview Ruby, because they need a social worker to sit in with that one. Normally it would be alright having her mother there, but as she's spilling the beans as well, they need someone else. Ironically they don't need someone with Leslie and she probably needs one more that Ruby.

Eventually, it seems like hours. It is hours. We are allowed home (that's my home) for the night. They consider that we may be in danger, so we have protection. This means we have a lovely Percy in the house with us and Barry and Pam outside in the arbour watching out for ... for... anything.

There's a postcard in the letter box and at first I think it is from Gandalf, but no it's from Suz on South Island in New Zealand.

Hello Nancy Old Girl,

Very green - lots of rain. You look at the mountains and think wow. Then you look up higher and there are the mountains - double wow. I am getting addicted to carrot cake. Everywhere you go it's carrot cake. Collecting great carrot cake recipes - 8 so far - yum, yum. Done the Hobbit Tour. Went Whale watching- probably saw the tail of a whale. They like dogs here.

Kia Ora (it's not just a drink), Suz xx

The big detective, not in size, but self importance, is quite rightly very concerned about Brenda and the other children in the house in Bastedge, but they don't want to just rush in and make things potentially worst. So they watch it. It's just like the telly. A van with cameras and things. They also take up a room in an old people's home at the back so that they can watch the garden.

I don't sleep well.

Another bloody postcard. This one is of the Rain Forest, Borneo from Suz Bedgegood.

Hello Nancy Old Girl,

Have been to Shangrila - really, it's in Borneo. Still more beaches. Orangutans surprisingly lovely. Food interesting - would appreciate a Big Mac. Weather unbearably humid. Pleased I brought my mac.

Still don't know how to say goodbye in Bornioese , but I would like to say goodbye to you and to Borneo- I *would love a cup of Earl Grey and a bit of cricket at Bastedge. No hearing dogs here.*

Suz xx

I could do with a couple of days in Borneo now.

We're taken to another police station this morning in cars that have all the full works of a police car - loads of gubbins and whistles and sirens and things.. Unfortunately they ignore my plea to have the siren on. I cannot reveal the location that we were taken to - this is all top secret. It's probably excitement I could do without. The seating in these places is pants and my hip is giving me gip. Ah well.

We are sitting like royalty at the top of a large conference room/ warehouse. We feel important and that all of a sudden people want to hear what we have to say and are not going to cross examine us.

Derek the self important man who I learn is god, runs the meeting. He welcomes us all to the briefing for Operation Funeral. The room is packed.

We are individually introduced. I am delighted to have my full title **Emeritus** Professor of Dentistry Nancy Byrde. I don't quibble with it being Emerita, 'cos I'm a woman, that seems like splitting hairs. The operations team are told that we will be at the Francine's funeral and that we should not be arrested, because we have been helping them, the police, with their enquiries.

I notice that there is an enormous board with like a family tree on it. We are all on it with our photos. I will ask if I can keep it after all this. Someone with an artistic bent who likes cutting and pasting had a field day with it. Don't know where they got my photo from, but it looks like a prison one. That makes some sense.

A police sergeant gives a lowdown on all individuals involved. Francine who will be in a box, Fintan the criminal mastermind, Bobby the American link (of course), Charlie the canal logistics manager. He does a short little speech about the Colonel and his early involvement in drugs running. No one knows where he is. It seems that the house in Florida where Bobby goes to stay was his at one time, but he gave it to Francine as a gift. How interesting! I am learning so much about this awful criminal side of the family. Leslie and Ruby don't seem too surprised by any of this, I think none of it is new to them. Chris is completely shocked. Then another copper gives details of all the monitoring they are doing, the comings and goings at the house in Bastedge.

Brenda sends me a text

Kids Ok. Flowers 4 Fri way in with florist? Netball x

I read the text out to the throng. Someone types it onto a laptop and it comes up on a large screen.

'Shall I text back?'

'Yes.' Says Derek. 'Ask her which florist?'

'We know - phone conversation at 9.37 am - it's Fresh As Daisy, Sir. It's in Moseley, Sir.' says a voice from behind a computer.

'Netball?' Says another voice.

'Code name.' I answer. 'Shall I just say thank you Brenda?'

'Yeh, say thank you - any other ideas? No, yes, just say thank you. Right, guys, the specific planning for Operation Funeral. Your brief is, that's you five - Leslie, Ruby, the Professor and her dog and you Sir - mmmmm Chris ummmm.... will arrive at the house at 10.29. You will walk behind the hearse to the Church. The service will go ahead. Then people will travel to the Crematorium. There will be police officers in mufti walking to the church, at the service and at the Crem. Our officers will go into the house with sniffer dogs as soon as the end of the funeral cortège rounds the corner by the Botanical Gardens. OK? Arrest will be made as Fintan, Bobby and Charlie leave the Crematorium. We are expecting others in the drugs underworld to attend, so further arrests may be made. The children in the house are being monitored from afar now. The children's Aunty Beryl is doing most of the caring. It is believed that Beryl Bird - different spelling of Bird than either Francine Byrde - she and the Professor have chosen a more sophisticated spelling - that is BYRDE. Where was I? Oh yes, Beryl the decease's sister has no criminal involvement. We believe. The children are Brenda 12, Basil or Baz 8 and 18 month old twins Barbara and Bertie Flannery. They will be checked over by social workers. Emergency foster care is very difficult at the moment, so currently we believe that Aunty Beryl will carry on caring for them probably at Professor Byrde's house.'

This is news to me.

Then the screen bursts into life.

'Here are some of the notorious criminals we are hoping to see.'

Faces flick up on the screen. The photos were of people you would not like to bump into on a dark night along the towpath on the canal. Included was the face of the nice man in lycra that I chatted to when the paint on the bench was fresh and the last face was of Geoff the angler.

Our bit of the briefing over we are free to leave, so we go to Solihull to pick up something smart and black to wear. Steven stays in the car for a kip, but we buy him a black satin bow. We still have our minders, Percy, Pam and Barry. They are lovely and appear to be nonjudgemental.

On the way back, Chris and Percy drop off at the boatyard to pick up the All Day Breakfast to bring it over to mine, because with those children and Beryl we will need to have more instant accommodation. Percy is very excited about a trip on a narrowboat, because he has never been on one before. Chris has promised him a go at the tiller.

Supper is easy tonight. Fish and chips. Steven is in heaven.

Funeral Friday is tomorrow.

Oh yes and a postcard has arrived showing that hotel The Burj Al Arab, Dubai from Suz Bedgegood.

Hello Nancy Old Girl,

It is all FAKE! I LOVE IT!

Elalleqa, Suz xx

PS - No Dogs!

Fake? Things are never what they seem.

Chapter Twenty Two

Funeral Friday is today.

People refuse sardines for breakfast, though I drop a couple in Steven's bowl. It is very important that Steven has his bowels open first thing, because the idea of a little message in Church does not float my boat. We go up the towpath very early. I'm still in my jamas under my mac. It is a beautiful day. Steven cleverly does a deposit in the canal and we see that there is no sign of Geoff the angler and all his equipment and tent have gone too. I can just see a yellow square of grass where his tent used to be from this side of the canal. Bench two is clear of paint and the empty message can is gone. I walk up to the rambling bridge and bench three. Lycra man is there. Only he isn't wearing lycra, but is wearing a neat black suit, white shirt and a black tie. His shoes are highly polished. This is man who is making an effort. I sit down next to him.

'Hello, how ya doing?' I say.

'I'm fine. It's early for you, isn't it?' He says.

'Yes, Steven needed a poo and what Steven wants, Steven gets.'

'Steven?'

'Yeh, Steven my dog.'

'That dog has a marvelous life, doesn't he? I wouldn't mind his life, really I wouldn't.'

'Yes, he does very well, but he deserves to do well, because he is a wonderful companion. He is my best friend, even though I have to ask him to put someone down sometimes.'

Lycra man laughs and it turns to tears.

'It's a sad day for me.'

'Oh I'm sorry about that. What's the matter?' I ask.

'My boss died a couple of days ago and she was very good to me.'

'Really.' I say. 'I'm sorry to hear that.'

'Yes, I've seen the world because of her.' He says.

'That sounds exciting.' I say.

'Yes, Miami in the US, Columbia, Pakistan, Albania, Ghana, Mexico, Afghanistan...'

'Oh, you were in the army?' I say.

'No, not exactly.'

'Travel broadens the mind, so they say.' I say.

'Yes, suppose it does. Anyway, it's her funeral today.' He cries again.

'I'm sorry you are so sad. It is good to have a fair boss.'

'Oh no, she wasn't fair.She was a cow, but no more jollies for me. The furtherest I'll ever go now is Barry Island. He, new boss man, will keep all the jollies to himself.'

'Life is all about change,isn't it? Who knows what will happen next? Must be getting back. Have a good day. Enjoy your funeral.'

I get back and the house is all activity. People showering and putting on their best bib and tucker. Black bib and tucker. And bacon sizzling for bacon sarnies. Leslie looks in a bit of a tizz.

'Are you ok, Leslie?' I ask.

'Yes.'

'Go on.'

'Well, She was a rotten bullying mother, Mother was, but she was the only mother I ever had. Wasn't she? She was, wasn't she? Now that she is dead and gone, I can relax and enjoy stuff and that is a good thing, isn't it? It is, isn't it? She won't just pop out of the blue and shout at me, like she did. But now I know that she will never be nice to me. She will never be kind, a proper mother, like mum's are supposed to be, That will never happen now 'cos she's dead. She's dead isn't she, so it is the sort of the end of the story, isn't it? She will never touch my hand in a gentle way. She will never say something like - Leslie that's a lovely picture, thank you Leslie for making me a cup of tea, Leslie you look beautiful in that cardigan. Those things will never happen now. It is the end of our story together. The end.'

'It is sad, but you can continue to be a good mother to Ruby and a fantastic new grandmother to Ruby's baby and that is what you have to think about.'

The taxi has arrived. Khaver has a black tie on, but he always wears a black tie. Chris got cold feet saying that he didn't know Francine. I told him that we needed him, even if he wears his tartan slippers for comfort with his new black suit. Ruby looks like a rock star in her black patent thigh high boots and Leslie was pleased to find a black twinset in M&S. I am wearing a black velvet little number with a black feather fascinator, lace fingerless gloves and Whitby jade earrrings. Well, it's a big little number in truth. Steven fits snuggly into the faux tiger skin bag, I bought. It is beautiful and I have learnt a new word 'faux' it means fake. There you are Suz - fake or faux like Dubai. If you half close your eyes and look at it with Steven in the bag, he could be taken for a little tiger cub with a cute black satin bow around his neck. Obviously he has a similar nature to a tiger, but without the teeth, but a dangerous suck.

Khaver takes us directly to Bastedge and it's a bit early so he drives around the one way system past the house. I put my hand up to the window and look through my fingers to gawp.

' There is a 1963 Buick Wildcat Convertible parked outside the house.' Says Chris.

'How do you know it's a 1963 Wildcat?' Asks Ruby.

'I just feel it in my water.' Chris says.

We drive around again in silence. All wondering why this iconic car is parked outside the house.

I check and it is 10.26. Time to park around the corner from the house, so that we can trot to the house for 10.29 am. All is good. We pile out and I see a coach has broken down parked on a double yellow line. Football supporters? No, police officers. The troops are ready to move in. We trot around the corner.

The Buick is now parked in the road. The back seat is overflowing with red, white and bluish flowers. There is no sign of the hearse.

And then we see it. The coffin is like one you see in American movies, red and shiny with enormous brass handles with two wreaths on top, one like the Union Jack and the other like the Stars and Stripes. The coffin is being carried by Fintan, Charlie, three ape men that look like bouncers, because they are wearing bow ties and tuxedos plus an erect, but elderly man in grey Army uniform with a red and gold ribbon on the cap.

This must be the Colonel.

They lay the coffin across the back of the car. What a way to go!

Leslie runs to the Colonel and hugs him. He seems pleased to see her and Ruby runs to them too. Bobby and Beryl are there suddenly with the children, Brenda looks splendid - just like a goth. The family all join hands across the road, stopping the traffic. Hundreds of people come out of the house joining in the parade and Chris and I wiggle in. Suddenly, there is the sound of a jazzband - 'When the Saints Go Marching In' I look around, but can't see it.

Then I realise it's coming from the Buick's radio. A bloke in drianpipes and a quiff gets into the driver's seat and starts the engine. The procession moves off. People put up umbrellas, New Orleans style and dance along to the Church. Barbara and Bertie open up a frog and a duck umbrella and wiggle their butts to the music.

This is not what I was expecting. I am reassured when I spot a couple I remember at the police briefing and then another.

As we approach the Church, we see crowds of people there applauding to welcome the body. We all pile into the Church past a nervous looking woman vicar who looks vaguely familiar. We are given order of services by two very large choir boys with large feet - police officers? The coffin stays outside on the car, because it will make a grand entrance. The organist is playing a familiarish tune and then I hear Chris singing - 'A Whiter Shade of Pale' under his breath. The Church is filled with white lilies and the smell hits you. Not a smell everyone likes.

I look at the order of service and there is a photo of Francine on the front. It was probably taken in about 1968. She is in her Mary Quant stage, before she became a hippy. Her hair is in an asymmetric bob and she grins at the camera. This is a very different Francine than the one I have ever known. It makes me sad to think that the promise in the photo was corrupted so badly. But then I think about it. I suppose I knew Francine when she did look like Twiggy and she might have looked like a model, but she was always a horrid manipulative cow. i remember the ice-cream incident. My birthday party, it must have been my seventh. Mum had set up a long trestle table. I am sitting opposite Francine. It comes to the jelly and ice-cream and Francine takes a spoonful of vanilla and splatters it into my face. Everyone laughs, except me.

The first page of the little booklet says

The focus of today's service is a celebration of the life of Francine Grace Byrde and her journey from earth to heaven.

There is no mention of hell.

The Church is packed. We are sitting near the back. I notice that the easiest way to exit is probably through to a side chapel. Maybe?

'Whiter Shade of Pale' is replace by a bit of Faure's Requiem and the coffin is carried in by the Colonel, Fintan, Charlie and the Bouncers. It looks very heavy indeed. I bet they wish they had a trolley. How heavy was Francine? The vicar with a choir of very large men and women who seem to be wearing surpluses that are a bit on the small side, lead the family in and they take the reserved seats in the front pews.

The vicar intones 'For I am convinced that neither death nor life, neither angels nor demons, neither the present nor the future, nor any powers, neither height nor depth, nor anything else in all creation, will be able to separate us from the love of God that is in Christ Jesus our Lord.'

I am happy that demons have a mention.

Then we are asked to sing the first hymn - Amazing Grace.

Amazing grace! How sweet the sound,
that saved a wretch like me!
I once was lost but now am found,
was blind but now I see.

The singing from such a large choir is pretty poor and I am trying to understand the words in the context of Francine Grace Byrde.

Then the vicar cracks on 'Welcome to you all today to this celebration of the life of Francine Grace Byrde. It is rare that this church fills to brimming with the family and friends of a loved one and it is a tribute to Francine that so many people have traveled from near and far to attend her special service of remembrance. Let us pray.'

I don't hear the prayer, because Brenda kneels on the pew and tries to get my attention. She waves her phone, I think at me. I look at my phone and there is a text message. My phone is on silent - we are in Church after all.

Overheard Uncle E - burners are his lot not the crems - why? xx

Burners? Well, it has to be something to do with burning the body - yes?

The vicar is droning on 'Support us, O Lord, **all the day long of this troublous life,**
until the shadows lengthen and the evening comes, the busy world is hushed,
the fever of life is over and our work is done. Then, Lord, in your mercy grant us a safe lodging, a holy rest, and peace at the last; through Christ our Lord. Amen'

It's time for another hymn -The Battle Hymn of the Republic it says on the service sheet and then the word - solo. The organist taps out John Brown's Body Lies A Mouldering In His Grave. The Colonel goes up to the lectern and in a clear strong tenor voice sings

Mine eyes have seen the glory of the coming of the Lord:
He is trampling out the vintage where the grapes of wrath are stored;
He hath loosed the fateful lightning of His terrible swift sword:

His truth is marching on.

No one joins in the chorus with him

Glory, glory, hallelujah!
Glory, glory, hallelujah!
Glory, glory, hallelujah!
His truth is marching on.

The Colonel with his cap under his arm, standing to attention, sings six verses each followed by six choruses. It is magnificent.

At the end, he stays there and gives us an eulogy.

'My dear Franny, I called my sweet lamb Franny, it being short for Francine, have been together from our first meeting at the US Airbase in Berkshire for... so very long. A very long time for a yankee to be married to the same woman. (Ha,ha, ha.) She looked sweet to me then when we first met, just as she did in her dying moments. You may be a wondering about the old Buick Wildcat out yonder and why my Franny is taking her last ride in it. Well, it's because it is the car that I drove her on our first date together.

Franny was a wonderful and resourceful woman, a terrific wife and a caring mother to our two fabulous daughters Roberta and Leslie. We have been blessed with five beautiful grandchildren who were the apple of her eye. Franny, well known in Birm-ing-ham for a charity work with the homeless, spent many hours in her role as counsellor. Our favourite moments together were just sitting at that big old kitchen table of an evening, sharing the stories of the day over a homecooked plate of something tasty that Franny had just rustled up for the whole family. I'll let you into a liddle old secret now. Franny learnt to make hominy grits just like my mama used to make, just for me.'

Hominy grits? Just disgusting.

'So now our dear Franny has gone from us. Gone to her maker. And we pray that he will receive her through those Pearly Gates with open arms. We must not grieve for her. We must take solace from the fact that she has completed her life's work with fortitude, selflessness and integrity. I'll love you forever, my dearest Franny. Amen.'

The Colonel reaches out heavenwards. He starts to sob. Holds onto the lectern for strength. Takes out a big hanky and blows his nose noisily. Then he goes to the coffin puts his hand on it. Bows his head and makes a silent prayer. Then steps back and salutes it. A fine performance.

I am completely flabbergasted. You could hear a pin drop. I don't think I was the only person to be shocked by this pack of lies. The vicar was looking very puzzled, she shot up and started the Lord's Prayer. A few people joined in. And then it was time for her sermon.

'It is now time for me to talk to you, the congregation about Francine. I was unlucky enough never to have met Francine, but I think the warmth of the Colonel's eulogy said it all, enough said. In the name of the Father, Son and Holy Spirit. Amen.'

The final hymn is 'Going Home'. No one knows it. No one sings.

Then the vicar says 'the service will continue at Lodge Hill Crematorium and all are welcome there, or please go to the Marriott Hotel at Fiveways for refreshments and an opportunity to share memories of Francine. To get to the Crematorium, you can take coach A that is waiting outside the church or to go to the Marriott take coach B. After the crematorium service coach A will take people to the Marriott.

You will all know that Francine had a deep love of contemporary music and her favourite band were the Verve. So we will take our leave to their music.

Everlasting God, comforter to the afflicted and healer to the broken, teach us the ways of gentleness and peace that all the world may acknowledge the kingdom of his son Jesus Christ our Lord.

The Lord shall preserve thee from all evil: he shall preserve thy soul. The Lord shall preserve thy going out and thy coming in from this time forth, and even for evermore. Amen.'

The vicar leads out the coffin, the choir and the family to the Verve. Later I found out that they were singing 'Drugs Don't Work'. I can see Brenda laughing like a drain.

I get my mobile out, so that I can ring Derek about the text from Brenda. I don't know what exactly it means. But it must be something to do with the cremation I think. My phone is dead. So I can't either send a text or speak to him.

'Have you got your phone, Chris?'

'Yes, thank you.'

'Can I use it? I've had a text from Brenda and I think I should pass the information on, so I need to speak to Derek.'

'You have Derek's number?' Asks Chris.

'Yes, but no, it's in my phone.'I say.

'I haven't got it, I'm afraid.' Says Chris. 'I didn't bother to get it, because you had it. Has Brenda got it? Leslie? Ruby?'

'Oh dear.' I could kick myself.

'This place is crawling with police. We could pass the information on to one of them. Right, let's play spot the copper.'

"I can't remember the message. What was it? Something that she overheard from mmmm Fintan. Something about new burners not the Crematorium ones. Oh dear. Brenda felt it was important and she's a clever girl. If Brenda thought it was important then I am sure it was. Where is she? Can we talk to her? We must talk to her.' I am so cross with myself.

'What are we doing now? We said we would go to the crem. The children aren't going there. I don't think they are. What shall we do?' Chris jumps from one foot to the other. He's anxious and so am I.

'Police officer. We need to talk to a police officer. Do you recognise anyone from that briefing meeting? Do you recognise anyone?' I say.

'I thought I did earlier. And earlier they all looked like coppers. You know, big feet and pointy heads to go up into those helmets.' Chris says.

'Come on. Let's pick one. I know we can do it. Which one? Look at that woman over there. The one with no dress sense. I put money on her being a copper. She has the shoulders. I'll go and start a conversation with her. What shall I say to her, Chris? Give me some ideas.'

"What about - are you a police officer?'

I go over to the shoulder woman.

'Excuse me, what a lovely service. Did you know the deceased well? You know, Francine? We were cousins. Not close, but still cousins.'

The woman seems preoccupied.

'I want to get a message to Derek. My mobile has died, so I can't use it and I don't know his number off hand. Do you know Derek?'

'Oh yes, I know Derek. Yes, I know him quite well. I can send a message to him for you.'

This is turning out to be easier than I thought.

'If you could send him a message to say that the burners have been changed at the crem.'

'That's an odd message. You are part of the funeral directors team then. I thought you must be, dressed like that. I'll send him a text for you now.'

She taps something into her phone.

'There you are, it's done. What a wonderful service. I love a good funeral, better than a wedding.'

Is this woman a police officer? I must have faith in the fact that she is and move on out to the crematorium and our transport problems are solved - we need coach A.

The heavens have opened since we have been in church. The glorious sunny day has been infected by lies and malice - the heavens are crying with relief that she has gone to the other place. Actually, I don't believe any religious rubbish. I'm an Atheist and proud. The others who dance with umbrellas in the parade before the service are fine because they can use them in the more usual way, but we get wet. The red coffin is put back on the Buick Wildcat, but it looks a bit dodgy in the rain. The three Bouncers are in the back in amongst the flowers. As the car moves off they put their arms over the coffin and keep it on board. A hearse might have been a better idea,

We run to the first coach. Yes, it has an A on the windscreen. We go to get on and Bobby, from the top of the stair, stops us.

'How dare you ruin my mother's funeral? You were not invited. Go away. You are getting on this coach over my dead body and I think one funeral is good enough for one day. You take my family away from me? You and your fancy man? Bugger off, Nancy. Shut the door, coach driver.'

I am really surprised that in that speech there was not one swear word. Such restraint.

Leslie and Ruby have their noses pressed to the glass and look sadly on and wave.

Chapter Twenty Three

The vicar gets into a Fiat Punto.

"Are you going to the crem? Can we have a lift?'
I ask.

'Where else do you think I'm going? Get in.'
She sounds really aggressive. We jump in. She
seems to be surprised that Steven is in my bag.

'Is that a dog?' She asks.

'Yes, it's Steven. He's my hearing dog. I can't
cope without him.' That shuts her up.

Her driving is aggressive too. She cuts up coach
A, she obviously wants to get to the crem first.
As she is driving she says ' you can't refuse to
do a funeral. You can say no to a wedding, but
you can't say no to a funeral.'

As a vicar, she has the best reserved parking
spot. She brakes into it, so we can just nip out of
the car and in. The crem is empty. We are the
first to arrive.We sit behind a pillar. We want to
avoid any confrontation with Bobby.

Something classical is being played on a CD
somewhere and again there is the smell of lilies.
This seems unlikely, because the flowers are silk
ones. The coffin hasn't arrived yet, the plinth for
it is exposed, the curtains drawn back ready for

the service. We hear the sound of a jazz band - it's the Buick's radio again. The vicar comes in and gets herself sorted at the front. The Bouncers have found a trolley and wheel the coffin in at great speed. One of them uses the coffin trolley as a scooter. Such fun. They throw Francine onto the plinth with no ceremony. The vicar is horrified and takes a sip from a glass of water.

We hear the coach arrive. People come in and it's like a day trip to Barry Island with laughter and chatter until people see the coffin and the little curtains. One by one - silence. There is the colonel, looking older now. He and Fintan were in deep conversation when they came in, but have now responded to the quiet. Bobby looks bullish. Leslie and Ruby looked relieved that there is no space for them in the front pews. I dodge around the column and they see me and hop back to share our pew. The children as planned are not here. Good.

It all happens super quick. The vicar is obviously late for her lunch.

She, the vicar speaks with authority and speed 'They shall suffer the punishment of eternal destruction and exclusion from the presence of the Lord and from the glory of his might, when he comes on that day to be glorified by his saints. This is our final farewell to Francine Grace Byrde. We commend Francine to God's love and mercy. We now commit her body to the ground; earth to earth, ashes to ashes, dust to dust: in the sure and certain hope of the resurrection to eternal life.'

With that the vicar leans forward and presses a button somewhere and the little curtain comes around slowly as the coffin sinks down probably to hell. It is certainly going to be burned.

'I am the resurrection and the life, saith the Lord; he that believeth in me, though he were dead, yet shall he live: and whosoever liveth and believeth in me shall never die.

I know that my Redeemer liveth...Amen.' The vicar has had enough. Sits and sinks into private prayer for a moment. Then jumps up and walks out, hissing at us as she passes 'I'm not going to the Marriott, so don't ask.' We hear the Punto rev up and scream out of the car park. So no lift for us then.

The Colonel, Bobby and Fintan lead the congregation out of the little chapel. Bobby spots Leslie, Ruby and I. She stops.

'What are you doing with her, Leslie? I've told you she is a dreadful woman. You will come with me now. Now that Mother has gone. I am in charge. That's me and Fintan. Come here now.'

'No, Bobby. I am a free person. I have free will. I do not have to do anything I don't want to. Nancy is my friend. She has been good to me and Ruby.' Says Leslie.

'Actually Aunty Bobby, we don't have to do anything you say. Mum is quite right. And we don't have to make explanations to you. We are only here today to make sure Granfran has gone forever. This is our final contact with you all. So goodbye.' Ruby has such a good way with words.

The Colonel takes Bobby's arm. 'Roberta, we have ways of working with people. We have control of this little situation. Come on my dear, we have plans to make and these people have shown that they have no sense of family loyalty. We must go now. Leave them here. They will live looking over their shoulder in fear.'

It's as though the air has frozen. Leslie and Ruby cling to each other.

As the last of the people leave we, Leslie, Ruby, Chris, Steven in his bag and me leave too. It is still raining. The coach is closing it's door and moves off. The next service will take place in minutes and a new set of mourners are stacking up to go inside.

We go and sit in the bus shelter.

'I'll ring Khaver to take us home? Take us to the Marriott? Probably not, but we can't stay here in the rain.' Says Chris.

'I had a text from Brenda' I tell Leslie and Ruby 'about Fintan's people being in place instead of the burners. Or somehting like that. My memory is shit. I can't show you 'cos my phone's dead. No battery. Let's think about that for a minute. Yeh, ring Khaver - it will take him ages to get here anyway.' I say.

'If Uncle Fintan has put his men into where the burners are.... This is a crematorium. It is where they burn bodies. Where do they burn bodies? There must be a fire somewhere here. Where Granfran's coffin went when the curtain came round. The coffin was travelling down somewhere. It must be where they burn her. It's all horrid, isn't it, but I think it is better than rotting in the ground for little stuff to eat you. Down below must be where the fire is. Does the coffin go straight into the fire? Probably not. If Fintan's got people there then maybe they want to burn it themsleves or something.... Shall we go and see what is happening now to the coffin?' Says Ruby.

We all know what she means. We are all reluctant.

The new mourners haven't gone inside yet, so we five all go back in. The curtains are still closed but the plinth has returned. I take Steven out of his bag. Ruby and he stand on the plinth. Ruby jumps up and down a bit. I remember that she is only 16. There is only room for the two of them. I press the little button and they go down. It moves down very slowly. I spot a door at the side and Chris, Leslie and I take a risk, maybe we can access the furnace this way? The door is unlocked and we go through it and go down a short stairway. Another door. You can feel the warmth through it. I suddenly feel fearful for Ruby and Steven. It opens easily. We go through.

The room doesn't remind me of the furnace room at my old school. We had a very nice caretaker when I was at school and if you wanted to bunk off lessons, you could go to the furnace room and have a cup of tea and a toasted tea cake with him. This furnace room looks like a laundrette with two big washing machines that are not places to do your smalls, but are places where you roll the coffin in and then press a button and everything inside burns. It isn't warm and cosy, but a functional space with an industrial edge. There is space where the lift shaft comes down. It is quite noisy from the gas burners in the two furnaces - it's a kind of roar. A couple of coffins are stacked to one side with Francine's red 'E' Type centre stage. Two women look in our direction, both are holding large pokers. I presume they are pokers. One of them is the woman I asked earlier if she was a police officer. I guess, she isn't.

'Sit down.' She indicates a coffin to sit on. 'Don't worry, we will say a prayer over your bodies as we put them in the furnace after we've taken you out. Out, yes, out.'

'I'm sorry there seems to be some mistake. We understood. We thought that we could come down and watch the cremation of Francine Grace Byrde. We just popped down. No problem at all. We'll just leave you to it.' says Chris as he stands up and makes for the door.

'You are not going anywhere' Says the other woman as she aims her poker at Chris. She has an American accent. 'Sit down now.'

'Before we kill you, You can help.' The woman with the American accent gives us instructions, but her accent slips. She has watched too many movies. I think she's a Brummie.

Help? Does she want us to put the bodies in the furnace? I'm not up for that, except Francine's, but not the others waiting for their turn in the other boxes. Francine - yes, at a push, because she is family.

"There are a load of used Sainsbury's carrier bags and you will put ten small bags into each carrier and then tie the handles of each carrier together. Then you will put ten of the carrier bags into each of these.'

We don't understand.

The other women pushes five old lady shopper bags, not dissimilar to Steven's, on wheels from the side of the furnace.

'Bags of what? From where?' I ask.

She opens Francine's coffin. There is no body. There is no Francine. It is filled with bags of white powder. White powder? Oh yes, white powder.

Leslie screams ' Mother! Mother? Where's my Mother!' She jumps into the coffin and starts throwing the little bags out. Looking for the body I presume.

All of a sudden both women start waving the pokers around dangerously as Steven and Ruby jump out from the coffin lift shaft. Steven growls and bares the space where his teeth should be. And Ruby takes on one woman. There's a swipe of both pokers, one hits Ruby across the back of the head, the other wounds her shoulder and Ruby falls. Steven rips a hand open and a poker falls to the floor. The brave little chap sucks the blood out of the other woman's calf. She is in pain and Chris wrenches the poker from her.

'She's pregnant. I've hit a pregnant woman.' The mock American is obviously a novice at drugs' running. I believe that the Byrde Drugs Empire is being stretched to its limit.

Chris takes both pokers and deposits them into the lift shaft and sends them up. Leslie rushes to Ruby's side. Blood is coming from her shoulder. I put her into the recovery position. We put Leslie's cardigan against the wound to stop the bleeding. Ruby is as white as a sheet. We are terrified. Chris dials 999.

The door opens and it's Khaver followed by lots of police. Khaver explains that he got to the Crematorium and parked in the car park. It was busy - lots of burnings today, so he had to go into the staff car park. He parked next to a green van and when he got out to look for us, because we weren't obvious, he heard banging and shouting coming from inside the van. Very rude words, it seems. Khaver wouldn't tell me what. Anyway, he opened the back door. It wasn't locked. Wasn't locked! And he found a couple of guys tapped up. Taped together. You know, that gaffer tape stuff. He undid them, but that was easier said than done. It's tough stuff. He had to get a knife out of the boot of the taxi. It seems they were quite wary at first. They thought he might be one of them. One of them who taped them up. Khaver was brandishing a knife. Anyway, he called the police and there they were. The police were crawling all over the place at the crem, but not necessarily where all the action was going on.

The police were just a little late to stop Ruby from being hurt. She has now lost consciousness. Leslie whispers lovely things in her ear. An ambulance comes and takes Ruby to the hospital. Leslie is not allowed to go with her. She has to go to the police station with us. She is distraught.

The police, who must have been around quite close, turn up in droves. Some in the riot gear and some in plain clothes. The ones in plain clothes are smart in suits smelling of Giorgio Armani with very shiny shoes.

We go with the police.

More accurately, we are taken by the police in a people carrier. Very comfy and I think Khaver would like one like it. They bring Khaver too. He is well miffed, 'cos he has an afternoon full of taxi trips already booked. They, the coppers, won't let him ring control to let them know, so there will be people waiting and he won't turn up. He is upset, because he is always reliable. Of course, he doesn't know anything about anything, except that a couple of blokes were taped up in the crematorium car park and that I am always up to something weird.

We are interviewed separately. Our interviews are formally taped. It is just like on the telly. There is a copper in uniform standing by the door. I'm interviewed by Derek, so I feel very important and he has a woman with him. She looks quite normal. Someone who you might see in the school playground. I tell them everything that I know. I have no real first hand knowledge. I know stuff because I have been told it. Leslie has to experience it all. She will be in a a mess worrying about Ruby. Our interviews are all taped on a little tape recorder. And it's funny 'cos when someone goes out or comes in, someone has to say it. I tell them everything that I have written down here. Everything that you have read that I have written down here. Though much of it is what others have told me. I have never seen Francine, nor Fintan nor Bobby for that matter do anything illegal, I don't think. I've never seen them sell drugs and except for the huge number of bags with white powder at the crem, I haven't seen any evidence of drugs.

I think they must be happy with us because they take us to the big conference room that we had the Operation Funeral briefing. And there are Brenda with Beryl, Baz, Barbara and Bertie. Beryl looks wretched. I still think she had absolutely no idea about her sister's drug empire. It must be a hell of a shock, because Beryl refuses to take a paracetamol for a headache. I tell Brenda what a brave girl she is and how proud I am of her. I give Beryl a big hug. She cries on my shoulder. I give the key to my house so that she can take the children there as they cannot go back to the Bastedge house, because of the continued forensic work going on. Beryl lives in a tiny flat in Harbourne - no room for her and four children, even though the twins are small. Swinging a dead cat comes into mind.

Fintan, Bobby, Charlie and others are under arrest. It will take the police some time to sort out who did what. Lycra man from bench three or Harry Box as he is otherwise known, is under arrest too.

The Colonel? What happened to the Colonel? Good question.

We are told that we are free to go. I want to hear all about the operation, every detail, but not now. We want to go to the QE to see Ruby. I pray, and I don't pray, that she and her baby are both alright. Poor vulnerable Leslie is withered and confused. She has shut down. She is finding it hard to talk and rocks herself gently. She needs to see her daughter as soon as possible.

Khaver is just leaving the police station too after his interview, so he drops us, Leslie, Chris and me off without a charge, which is very kind. He also takes Steven with him. He promises to take the little dog home to Mrs Khan. She will feed him the tinned sardines that are in the bottom of his bag. Dogs are not welcome at the hospital, though I know that Ruby would love to see Steven. I change my mind. Steven will come with us. No one will know he is there in the lovely faux tiger bag. He always cheers people up. People, that is, who he hasn't attacked. I thank Khaver very much and ask him to pass on my regards to Mrs Khan.

We know our way to the intensive care ward. Ruby is on the same place as her grandmother was.

'Hello again.' One of the nurses walks pass.

We ask permission to go on the ward and I say that Lesley is Ruby's Mum and that I am Ruby's Aunt. I'm told that someone is with Ruby and that she is only allowed two people with her at the time. I don't know who to expect, but Leslie needs to be by Ruby's side and whoever is there must move out for me.

As Ruby and I enter. I can see who it is by Ruby's bedside in full uniform. It's the Colonel. I turn back and tell Chris to ring the police, his second 999 call of the day. And then I go back. Leslie has disappeared.

'Hello Colonel. We met very briefly, I think in the early 70's. 1973? '74? I'd like to say that it's good to see you again.'

"Ah Nancy Byrde. It was good to see you today from afar. You were always a goodlooking kinda gal. You were my favourite, you know.'

'No I wasn't, don't try your bullshit on me. That was a terrific performance in church. I didn't recognise the Francine, oh yes, Franny from your description. I wasn't aware that you see her very often.'

'You don't know nothing Nancy Baby. Me and my Franny see each other all the time. Those long holidays in Miami and other places too. I may not have been able to get into the UK, but Franny could always get out. Anyway, who wants to be in the UK with the weather here. I have a worldwide empire now and Francine managed the UK enterprise very well for many years. Me and my darling Franny have had a long and fruitful marriage.

Of course it's probably Fintan's now, taking over the reins. Probably. I'd like to have given it to Bobby? But she's too headstrong. She does first and then thinks later. Leslie is simple in the head, so no joy there.'

I notice Leslie is hiding under the bed.

'What are you doing here Colonel? Here at Ruby's bedside?'

'Well, I still hold out a little hope for Franny's preferred heir. Ruby is blood. Ruby is bright, except for the bastard she's carrying. Ruby has an independent spirit. She's nice with people too and that's important. Never underestimate the importance of charm in the drugs trade, Nancy. It is the key factor in my success.'

'But you didn't get to the wedding, Colonel - Bobby and Fintan's.'

'I got to host the other ceremony the one in Miami. Fintan's mother doesn't fly so there had to be some sort of ceremony here. I hear you were the star turn.' The Colonel laughs unkindly.

'They will always remember it at the Mandalay Bay. It was the best wedding ever. They still talk about it.'

'Utter humiliation for you, of course. Anyway, I understand from the nurse that people who are unconscious can often hear. So, I've put my plan to Ruby.'

'Your plan?'

'Yes, my plan is that Ruby should get better. Have the bastard. Farm it out and then take over the enterprise from the Bastedge house. The network with the logistics works well. Then when things are good here, we need to develop new markets and a young woman of her calibre and charisma is the way to go.'

'Doesn't she, Ruby, have a say in all this?'

'Of course, Fintan won't like it nor will Bobby but... and it would be hard as a single mum running a business of this size, but we can fix that. Ruby was Francine's preferred heir and she is mine. It means hard work, imagination, but huge financial rewards. Money isn't everything in life, but it oils the wheels nicely. It gives you more options and power.'

'Perhaps prison too.' Leslie pops out from under the bed.

'So there you are. Poor little junky Leslie. Leslie who couldn't say 'no'. Leslie with the bad habit. What are you doing under the bed? I hope you're not hiding from me, your Papa. Because, let's be honest, I don't care for weak people. With your genes, you should have been a strong woman, but no. You are just like my bellyaching mama who didn't do nothing, but whine and moan. But your kid, Ruby, here, Leslie. She has a brain. Ah well, Ruby my dear the empire can be yours, because you have grit and my brains. You can take it all on when you get out of this bed.'

And with that Ruby does. She gets out of bed.

'No I can't and I won't because I have a moral code. It is not just illegal, Action Man,yes Action Man, you were never a proper soldier. It's just a bloody front. It's immoral giving people junk to ruin their lives. It's wicked to, to make someone dependent on shit. To make them turn against their family and commit dreadful crimes to get a stash. I hate you with a vengeance for what you allowed to happen to my mum, who is worth thousands of you.' Ruby is shaking with rage.

The Colonel, no I have decided to call him the Colon, as he is a bit of a bowel and not really a military man. The Colon is now sitting down on his butt.

Derek the senior cop guy comes in followed by the nurse.

'You cannot come onto the ward, you are not a relative and there are already two by the bed, Two? No three? No, Four. You should be in bed young lady. Then there should be no more than two by the bed and those should be relatives or close friends. A dog! And absolutely no dogs!' Says the nurse.

'He's a hearing dog.'

'I am very please he can hear me, but I don't care if he's one of her majesty's corgis, he's not allowed in here. He is definitely not sterile!'

'I am arresting you for entering the UK illegally, but there are other charges against you. Come this way, Sir. Take him away, Jackson.' Derek speaks to a posse of coppers who have turned up from nowhere.

'Get your hands off. This is the uniform of an officer in the Unite States Army. I will be talking to the Ambassador. I will be talking to the President. I have the ear of the President. We go back a long way....'

The colon's voice trails off as he is taken off by police men. Good riddance, I say.

'Is the baby Ok, Ruby? I didn't want to ask, but the baby, please say he's, she's Ok.'I ask.

'Everything is Ok and I should be home very soon. Home? Well, out of hospital.' Says Ruby.

'Come to mine, Please come to mine. And Derek there are just two things I need to know, before you go.' I say.

'OK.' He says.

'Flowers - did your people go into the house in Bastedge as florists?'

'Oh yes, lots of sneezing went on. Beresford has hayfever. They had a very good snoop around when they went in. And no luck, there was no evidence of any illegal drugs or drug manufacturing, that they could see. Of course that's before the forensic team went in. We were monitoring the toing and froing from a chip van we had parked outside.

We think they probably put all the stuff in the coffin after they gave us a shipping order for cod and chips times sixteen and we had none to sell. They must of realised that we were not a chippy and that they were being watched. ' Derek explains.

'That brings me to my next question - where is Francine?'

'Good question. She's buried in the garden under an apple tree. A nice place to spend eternity I think. We believe that the boys, well, men, probably Fintan with those bouncer types buried her there last night. The sniffer dogs went straight to the spot when they went in after all the fun and games this afternoon. The boys thought it might be a stash of crack cocaine, but no, after they got through the layers of bubble wrap, it was the body of an old woman.'

The nurse comes back in with her knickers in a twist ' I can count you know. There are three people round this bed and that is one too many.'

'I'm off now, my dears and we have room for you at mine.' I leave the hospital with Steven and Chris. The nurse has forgotten that Steven is a dog with all the police invading her space.

Chapter Twenty Four

More than a postcard from Suz Bedgegood

Good to be back home. Traveling is tiring. But it has taught me so much.

The trip started two months ago. The initial crossing of the city was hell. Arrived late, of course. The rucksack seemed a good idea, but I wished early on for a little suitcase with wheels. When I left home it was all about looking like a world traveller rather than saving my back. Changed the bag. Found a nice little hard silver one in a sale. Bought it and took everything out on a bench outside, repacked and dropped off the rucksack with someone begging. Good call Suz.

Got up to the water and had a cuppa looking out. The tea was disappointing. Very grey, both the sea and the cuppa. No tip. No one gets a tip from me without some effort.

Walked around. Needed to stretch the old legs. Stopped off at a second hand bookshop. Was tempted, but thought - no.

Walked back to the front. Booked in. Third floor, but there is a lift, slow but safe. There is a view of sorts. Don't want to come all this way and not have a view. I can see a bench down on the front - very handy.

Room inspection. Cleanliness - pretty good by modern standards. Took out my squirter and fresh j cloth and gave the surfaces and the mirrors a good going over. Used the toothbrush on the taps and then a thorough cream cleanse of the bath and the toilet. Up to Suz's acceptable standard. Not Suz's Gold Standard - no evidence of beeswax polish. Forgot to pack my own. Not like me. Should have brought some with me. Will get some tomorrow. Then the room will smell of home.

Chipped paintwork around the door. Floor tile in the bathroom is slightly off - done without a spacer, I suspect.

Made another cuppa, this time with a biscuit in the room. It has a small kettle and something called creamer - ??? This time the colour of the tea was almost acceptable. Decent teabags must go on my list. Two in a little packet - biscuits that is. Kept one for later. Teabag naked, not in a little bag with a string - good. When you want tea, you want it immediately. Must buy a small bottle of semi-skimmed too.

Pleased there is a bath, not just a shower. How do you wash your lady bits properly when the water comes down? Your bits need to soak. There is a shower over the bath. You have to switch the bar over, up for bath, down for shower.

Unpacked. Not enough hangars. Rang down for some more. Am told I have the required number. There is a certain number for each room. Tell them that I require more.

Had a lie down. Played with TV - not very good. Missed Countdown. Slept.

Woke up and had a bath. No little sachets of stuff - very disappointing. Rang down - am told there is a machine that I can get them from. Call this service.

Got dressed in linen suit - very international and went down and sat on the bench. It was vacant. Checked before going down. The sea is still grey and the seaweed is in vile piles. There is a strong pong, because the wind is coming off the sea in my direction.

Very quiet. Just a few lone joggers. A few lone joggers? A girl in pink wired up to big headphones, a man in short shorts who looked ready for a heart attack and a woman in PE kit in a wheelchair with a yorkie on her lap spinning the wheels so fast.

Bought a strange kebab thing from a takeaway. Was desperately hungry otherwise wouldn't have bought it. The place looked reasonably clean though. Took it to my room to eat. Binned it - very greasy. Then took it out of the bin and took it to the seagulls outside. They are undiscerning unlike me. Hot chocolate before bed. Nasty sachet left in the room - there was nothing Belgian about it.

Disturbed night. Mattress not up to scratch and rowdy people in the corridor outside, until I shouted.

Breakfast buffet. I'll give them breakfast buffet.

Went for a walk. Needed beeswax, teabags and decent biscuits. I wanted to go to that second hand bookshop again.

A windy day, pleased I had brought my four season anorak with all the pockets. Used all the pockets for essentials, leaving hands free for shopper. Brought my hand fold away shopper - no need to use retailers' plastic bags - good gal, Suz.

There are very many dogs here. They are not casual dogs, but pedigree. All are on leads attached to an owner or a professional dogwalker. They have owners who don't talk to them, though the dogwalkers do. They obviously do their job, because they love the animals. All of the dogs are well groomed and have finely made leather collars. The outdoor cafes have bowls of water and a dogs' place is defined clearly. The beach is out of bounds to the right of the pier. Everywhere you go there is dog signage and little bins for their mess that seem to be emptied from time to time.

Whilst out bought decent teabags, marigolds, ginger biscuits, but no beeswax available at all, anywhere, so got a lavender squirty polish which will have to do and some serious bleach. Bleach is always useful.

Then I went back to the second hand bookshop. Heaven, except, of course, it's not clean. Hence the marigolds. Found a lovely atlas, but too pricey and of course out of date. And there it was again. No one had snapped it up. A beautiful scrap book full of postcards from around the World. Before negotiating a book price with a comatose youth on work experience, I checked to see if the postcards had been written on. They hadn't, so I pushed the boat out and spent £17 on it. The going rate for a postcard is between 40p and a pound, so I think a collection of 40 odd postcards for £17 is not bad plus I get the scrapbook too.

When I got back to my room, I give the scrapbook a spray with my disinfectant atomiser.

The room had been cleaned. No, it hadn't at all. The bed had been made and, yes, they had used hospital corners.The tea tray had been replaced with a new set of cup, saucer, nasty teabags, sachet of coffee and hot chocolate, but the biscuits had not been replaced. Maybe, you only get a little packet when you first arrive?

The cleaning regime is not that thorough, unfortunately. Before leaving my room to go out, I tore off a fragment of paper from the teabag and put it on behind the door of the bathroom. It was still there. Whoever was allocated cleaner to my room, had not seen the offending litter.

Anyway, before setting to with the postcards, I had a systematic clean through and used the lavender squirt. Not beeswax, a poor substitute, but beggars can't be choosers as my mother used to say.

I checked that the bench was clear before taking my postcards to the sea front. It wasn't but I guessed that if I sat with determination on the spare end, I could probably clear it pretty quickly. I can see that the person who is sitting there has a large pink pushchair. I presume from that the child seated in it is a girl as everything is gender specific nowadays. I understand from the Guardian that everything is pink for girls now and that there is no choice. No wonder feminism seems to have come to a miserable end.

I travel down and out. I have trouble crossing the road. The traffic is hell. Fancy coming out for a day trip and then spend the whole time looking for parking. I am very pleased that I have swopped the car for a new refridgerator. I should have got more for it, but secondhand cars do lose their value.

The faded young woman with the child in the pushchair finished her cigarette and ignores the child. I am unhappy that she leaves the cigarette end on the ground. I feel a tremendous urge to pick up this dog end, but as my marigolds are up in my room, I didn't feel that I can do this. I promised myself that I will come back down some time later with my marigolds so that I can put the offending litter in the nearby municipal bin. Though it will almost certainly be picked up by the early morning gulley sucker. Is it a gulley sucker? Or do I mean a giant hoover. It is generally very effective.

I looked at the postcards with great interest. I looked carefully at each picture and I read the usually limited information on the back. They are not stuck into the scrapbook, but each one is kept in place with little triangular corners, just like the ones my father used in my childhood photo albums. My father was a keen amateur photographer, turning our bathroom into a studio with a red lightbulb.

I sat on that bench for sometime at the beginning of my stay in the South Coast. I decided that I would send cards to friends. I looked through my address book and it comes down to Simon and Nancy. I worked with Simon for many years. He was deputy head and he tried very hard to always do the right thing, but he had only taught in one school, so he didn't know what the full range of possibilities could be. Poor Simon with his smelly armpits and a poor sense of personal hygiene. I think he hankered after me a little, but I could never be attracted to someone who felt no urgency in changing his underwear. Anyway, we stay in touch through proper snail mail and an occasional phone call. And of course, I've known Nancy for years. No idea how we first et, except it was back in the mists of time. She is such a good sort really, though she really should put down that little runt that stinks of fish, has explosive wind and toxic breath.

I tried to work out two world tours using the cards. Simon and Nancy don't know each other so they won't compare itineraries. This proved very difficult in the open air, so I went back to the room and put the cards on the bed and tried to work out a sensible step by step journey, in fact, journeys. I started in New York for Nancy and Oslo for Simon.

So I set about writing and sending off the cards, one by one. The weather was changeable that summer as it always is, but I wrote most of the cards on that bench, only writing in the room if the weather was really inclemant.

For my last two nights in Eastbourne, I moved out of the Travellodge and moved into the Royal, almost next door. The Royal is so refreshingly sophisticated and European with Eddie from Amsterdam in charge. Except, of course, they welcome dogs. Had breakfast with a Chow and a sausage dog called Rolo. Anyway, loved the Royal and even with the dogs, I came home feeling I had at least done Europe.

Chapter Twenty Five

So we are putting up the Christmas tree, it's the top of a fir tree from the garden that needed a bit of haircut. Ruby used Chris's chainsaw to top it off. I have all the old decorations that haven't been out of the box for years. When you are on your own, you don't bother but now, well the children and family that I have always avoided have caught up with me.

This will be Ivy's first Christmas of course. She is living on the All Day Breakfast with her mum Ruby and GranLes. Of course Ivy is the first and probably the last baby to be born on the All Day Breakfast. How appropriate that a child who loves her food and likes to eat all the time, was born on a boat called the All Day Breakfast. It seems just right. It's moored at the front door. Chris is bunking in with me which is rather lovely. We don't make promises or any of that malacky. We don't need too. We are just very comfortable together.

Brenda spends lots of time here, but she is now back in the big house in Bastedge with her brothers and sister under the eagle eye of Aunty Beryl, who is a good sort. Really, she is. She had no idea about the drug business. She thought they were importing Fairtrade knick-knacks for sale at Farmers Markets and such like. She has had one hell of a shock, but didn't think twice about taking on four children. The children are quite needy, of course, because they have been neglected and are puzzled about what has happened. Beryl gives them time and listens. Good old Beryl. Her flat is too small for a family, of course, so as soon as the police had finished with it, she moved into the big house in Bastedge. It may have to be sold - you know bought with bad money, but they are OK so far.

Everyone is coming here for Christmas Day, that's including Geoff the angler, too. I s'spect he might be Ruby's other parent, but no one is saying. No one is saying very much about Geoff. Whatever is his past and his involvement, he is working hard at doing the right thing now.

I am also expecting Suz Bedgegood. Well, she doesn't have anybody. She has cut her world tour and returned home. After all there is nothing very exciting happening out there. It is all happening here. I didn't want her to come for Christmas, but...I have so much, I should share it. I hope she doesn't bring any photos.

I have noticed that all the postcards from Suz have British stamps on them and where posted - well, it looks like Eastbourne.

One of the things I keep thinking about it is who is Ivy's dad? I don't know. I'm pretty sure it's not the nice boy who travels up and down on the coal boat. He pops in all the time, not just on the boat, but often on a bicycle too. He is keen and Ruby blushed a lot when he is around. Parenting is less about genes, more about who's doing the job. and he's lovely with Ivy.

Ruby has taken to parenting like a duck to water, which is appropriate because she is now living on a boat. She is thinking about how she is going to support herself, Leslie and the glorious Ivy. She needs to return to her education and I'm sure she will at some point. Perhaps dentistry is the way forward. I'll talk to her about that. Good money in people's mouths and great opportunities for flexible working for a single parent.

Leslie spends most of her time around Ivy. She insists on hand washing her clothes. She is anxious to please and the doctor is giving her stuff to calm her down. So it's sadly back to drugs, I suppose.

For the Christmas dinner, I'm cooking a goose that Chris caught on the canal - don't be silly. No, we are not, we are going to eat a defrosted bird from the supermarket, like most other people. I did think about getting Geoff to catch a pike and keeping in clean water in the bath for a week to get rid of all the toxins and filth in its system and then eating that for Christmas dinner like they do in Poland, but it would only be me and Steven eating it.

Oh yes, and Steven, he's still the same old Steven. He is in heaven with all the attention he gets.

For the meal, I've made homemade ice-cream for pud, because no one fancies Christmas pudding. The pantry is loaded with food. I'm not used to all this catering. Steven and I have bought a box of kippers as a special treat and to make up for the loss of the Pike. I don't think any of our visitors will want to join us for those. Steven and I still love a good kipper. And sardines. I'm thinking maybe a bit of smoked haddock for tea later....

I don't think I have mentioned it, but I love a good read. Well, I used to like a good read, before all this happened. I like Jodi Picoult. You know the woman who writes great stories about big moral dilemmas - excellent. Well, her books always end with a court case. have you noticed? Always a court scene and I love them. Are you looking for the court scene here now? Well, of course there has been an enormous court case. It's been reported on the telly. Hit the national media. I had a very unflattering photo on page three of the Sun. I think they put it there, because it made the young thing next to me look very good. You maybe know more about it than me - the court case I mean. I know about what happened to me, but the court case? I only know about my bit of it.

I gave evidence. They wanted to know about finding Ruby in hiding in the bender and about the fracas at the crem. The Audi incident never came to light, so that must be our secret. I think we probably committed a criminal act, but it was small beer in comparison with all the other stuff done by others. The defense barrister in her wig and gown was very unpleasant to me and kept on approaching the bench and I have no idea really about what she was saying, but.... But she soon learnt you don't dice with me and that I can give as good as I get.

In the New Year, maybe we will do a trip to HMP Drake Hall to see Bobby, yes that is a good idea probably. I don't think we will be going to HMP Hammingbrum even though it's just up the road. Everyone is still very scared of Fintan. Even behind bars, everyone is scared of him. Charlie is doing OK at HMP Hewell. It's an open prison - that seems an odd thing, doesn't it? Charlie spilled the beans when he knew he had no option, so he didn't cop it too badly. And now he's in HMP Hewell, so close to the Cesterrow and Hammingbrum Canal that he went up and down on on the Lazy Daze, taking his illegal load from Bristol to Brum.

And then there is the Colonel. The Colonel is banged up in some high security place waiting for extradition to the States. He played the confused old man with Alzheimer's in the court. He's a very good actor or is he? I know that he's wicked and crazy and perhaps he has dropped into dementia.

Francine's body was cremated eventually. And her ashes have been scattered around the tree where she was bubble wrapped. Because of all the shenanigans, there was an inquest. They came up with natural causes - heart attack. Was there a suspicion of barbiturates? Francine sold drugs after all. No one suspected murder. No one has thought that a dentist, even a retired one could have access to lethal drugs. No one has suspected foul play. So that is alright then.

The bench with the dead lilies beyond the footbridge has fresh flowers now. Still white lilies and the same message.

To My Beloved Dai,   I am sorry and I don't blame you. If only we could go back in time, love Mum x

Geoff tells me it's the anniversary. It's the eighth anniversary of Dai's death. He was just 17 when he came up from Cardiff looking for his dad. Didn't find him, but found new friends. He used to drink rough cider with his mates during the day. No work, except for a bit of selling on the side. They sat on that bench and yes, it was rough cider during the day and other things in the dead of night. If you look in the brambles that grow up the wire fence, you can see needles in amongst the cans and bottles. So another year has gone, since he was found slumped on the flower bench.

Oh yes and my bench. Steven and I take our constitutional there every morning for a milk and a dash at about eleven. Chris usually comes with me, if he's not dicing the veg for the lunchtime soup and sometimes the others come too. Geoff has taken up angling properly and always waves and sometimes comes and joins us. There are no words on Bench Two now, I've put a wreath of holly around it for Christmas and I've planted some snowdrops around it. Ivy needs to be coaxed to grow around it too. A job for spring. After all this story started then and there. And who wrote those awful words on my favourite bench? I'm still working on that.

© Jan Watts
December 2012

Acknowledges

Thank you to my first dear reader, Jonk and then to Alan and Jan Cooper, Mervyn Vickery and David Wake. A special thanks to Linda Carter for reading the novel twice and for the wonderful lino print for the cover.

Lightning Source UK Ltd.
Milton Keynes UK
UKOW06f1259210716

278922UK00002B/173/P